STONE COLD

FOX

STONE COLD FOX TRILOGY
BOOK THREE

max monroe

Fox

A Stone Cold Fox Novel

Published by Max Monroe LLC © 2018, Max Monroe

ISBN-13:978-1986763868
ISBN-10: 1986763862

This is a work of fiction. Names, characters, places, brands, media, and incidents are either the product of the author's imagination or are used fictitiously. The author acknowledges the trademarked status and trademark owners of various products referenced in this work of fiction, which have been used without permission. The publication/use of these trademarks is not authorized, associated with, or sponsored by the trademark owners.

Editing by Lisa Hollett, Silently Correcting Your Grammar
Formatting by Stacey Blake, Champagne Book Design
Cover Design by Peter Alderweireld
Photo Credit: iStock Photo

DEDICATION

To Skittles: Not only do you taste delicious, but you also have a gross commercial that allows us to doomsday-parent our children into believing they can actually turn into a Skittle if they eat too many.
We really appreciate the help.

To Boxer Briefs: Thank you for highlighting the line of a cock perfectly yet seductively. You make character underwear selection so easy.

And to Levi and Ivy: Although you're not real, in our hearts, you are. Thank you for taking us on this journey. Your story was painful and hard and took us on a hell of a ride, but God, it is so damn beautiful.

FOX
BOOK THREE

Some things are meant to be; some *aren't*.

I never thought this would be my life.
I never believed I could feel this way.

I don't know where to go from here.
I never want to be anywhere else.

My whole world has changed.
She is my whole world.

I'm not sure how to be me again.
I've never felt more like myself.

I've never needed anyone, but I need him.
I love her. I'll always love her.

But is our love enough? Can Levi and I really survive this?
Together, Ivy and I can survive anything.

PROLOGUE

Levi
March 28th, 2016

M Y HEART THRUMMED PAINFULLY AS I PULLED IVY CLOSER TO MY
chest and put my lips to her hair.

She was silent, and the expression on her face couldn't
be described as anything other than lost. Jagged red lines broke the
smooth white surface of her eyes, and an angry blush swallowed up
the normally perfect skin of her cheeks. Her body was in the throes
of a meltdown.

But that wasn't a surprise. Half of her soul—Camilla's half—
had been severed and battered and was, right then, struggling to hold
on through a set of trauma doors and unyielding concrete walls.

As identical twins, Camilla and Ivy were bound together by ties
that were supernatural and inexplicably complicated.

They'd been born of the same egg, housed in the same mother,
and lived a cherished life together. But now, they'd been forced to
fend for themselves. Camilla fought for her life, and Ivy was left to
stand by and do nothing.

I knew the torture of helplessness. I'd known it with Grace, and
now, I knew it all over again as I watched Ivy lock herself inside and
completely shut down emotionally because she couldn't aid in the

physical fight for her sister.

"Levi," the chief greeted, his voice softened by grief. He gave me an affectionate squeeze of the shoulder with one hand and continued to hold his wife closer with the other.

They'd just arrived, the first of the crowd of support I knew would gather at Ivy's and my sides. Margo had been sobbing on the way over here—I could tell by the mottle of her face and throat and the moisture in her eyes—but she'd pulled it together before entering the building for the sake of Ivy and for the sake of the town.

We were well-versed in disaster. Our strength, it seemed, was in our ability to stand beside one another despite it.

I noticed the dried blood that coated my hands as I smoothed them down the rigid lines of Ivy's arms and pulled her even closer.

She was in shock; had been since the moment I'd abruptly woken her from a sleep aid-enhanced slumber and told her the news that had brought us here.

Cool blood still lay on the floor of the house we'd left, and police still swarmed over the bodies of Boyce Williams and Dane Marx, collecting evidence.

But the blood could wait. It would wait until we had word on Camilla, and Ivy had anything and everything she needed.

From this moment on, I was a man at her disposal. I'd be her punching bag when she needed and her shoulder to cry on when she allowed. For her, I vowed to be anything and everything. *Always.*

Moments after it had all gone down, mere seconds after I'd fired a bullet straight between Boyce Williams's eyes, I'd been unwilling and unable to admit to Camilla's end. Not there, next to the man she'd been willing to face head on in an effort to protect her sister. Not in the house where she'd spent those moments in terror, waiting for me to save her.

Not while her sister slept unwittingly in the next room.

And now, all I could do was pray.

FOX

Pray for Camilla. Pray for Ivy. Pray for a fucking miracle.

The door to the trauma unit opened swiftly, and a doctor came through, still pulling her mask from her face. Her surgical scrubs were covered in blood, and the look on her face would be burned into my mind for the rest of eternity.

"Camilla Stone's family?" she asked, bone-weary and broken.

I knew the words before she spoke them. I'd lived them before. But Ivy, *sweet fucking Ivy*, still had a relationship with hope.

She hadn't seen Camilla before the ambulance took her.

"Yes." Ivy's voice was scratchy and dry from the screams and wails and subsequent nonuse. Her agony had been physical as I'd told her the news. Potent. Piercing. "That's me. I'm her sister," she said. "And our parents are in LA, but they're trying to catch a red-eye flight out here."

My throat thick with saliva, I did my best to steady myself, hooking my arms around Ivy's body.

I knew when the words came—words that would change everything she'd ever known—she'd need the support.

Direct and professional, the doctor stepped forward to Ivy and made eye contact, but she worried the mask in her hand with her fingers. "I'm Dr. Ines," she introduced herself, and Ivy nodded and swallowed, unable to say anything else.

"Your sister came in with a severe laceration to her throat and had lost a significant amount of blood volume. We rushed her to the operating room, started a transfusion, but we lost her on the table. We defibrillated for twenty minutes, but I'm...I'm sorry. She didn't make it."

High-pitched and soul-destroying, the wail Ivy let out was the likes of which I would never recover from. It keened and moaned, and utter devastation rattled at its core.

She was a half of a whole now, and she'd never find the missing piece.

"Oh, Ivy," I murmured, pulling her close and spilling into the abyss of guilt.

The bottomless pit of blackness that taunted I could have done something more—that I could have stopped it if I'd taken it all more seriously from the beginning.

Hell, I hadn't even told Ivy the heroic decision Camilla had made to protect her.

But it wasn't out of secrecy; it was because I knew, in this moment, Ivy wouldn't be able to handle the truth of her sister's sacrifice.

God, I'd give anything to change this, to remedy the pain Ivy would never release, but I was powerless.

Helpless to alter the past and unable to protect the future.

All I could do was live this *with* her, be present *for* her, and pray for God's grace.

We couldn't take any more hits.

We couldn't take any more surprises.

Though, as the ones left behind—no matter what came—we had no choice but to survive.

And I'd spend the rest of my life making sure we did it *together.*

THE NEW YORK POST
Lightning Strikes Twice

Two days ago, tragedy once again rocked the small town of Cold, Montana. After six years of peaceful quiet followed the string of murders carried out by the Cold-Hearted Killer, Camilla Stone, Hollywood starlet Ivy Stone's twin sister, and the circumstances of her death have brought Cold back into the news.

March 30th, 2016

COLD—Authorities say just six years after the killing spree that took Montana by storm transpired, another set of tragic deaths has occurred.

Cold, Montana has been the home to Hollywood's finest for the last few months while **the truth-based film, *Cold*, was being filmed. The script is based on the real-life events of Grace Murphy, the police detective killed in the line of duty while investigating the Cold-Hearted Killer.**

On the evening of March 28th, popular Hollywood actress Ivy Stone and her sister, Camilla, were in their remote rental house in Cold, under the watchful eye of an active police officer Dane Marx, following several incidents related to Ivy's stalker.

Boyce Williams, a producer on the film, texted Ivy Stone to confirm her whereabouts and then used that information to carry out his plot.

Officer Dane Marx was killed at the scene, while Camilla Stone was transported to Cold Medical Center for immediate

attention. She was declared dead an hour later. Ivy Stone, said to be sleeping in a back bedroom of the home, was unharmed.

"To say this has rocked us would be an understatement," Chief Pulse said during a press conference. "The loss of one of our officers, combined with the tragic death of one young woman while visiting our community, is overwhelming. We're doing our best to cope and make sense of something like this happening here again."

"Boyce Williams showed unusual behavior throughout the filmmaking process," Officer Levi Fox of the Cold Police Department admitted at the press conference. "None of us saw an ending like this, though," he concluded.

Levi Fox is the officer responsible for killing Boyce Williams after finding Dane Marx dead, and this isn't his first foray into the news. Six years ago, Officer Fox was also the one to take the life of Walter Gaskins, thus ending the months-long reign of the Cold-Hearted Killer.

The city's medical examiner is in the process of performing autopsies on both of the victims, and details will be forthcoming. All of this has the town of Cold on high alert and its citizens fighting for a resolution. "We're a quiet town of quiet people," Lana Jessup, a longtime resident commented. "We're ready to get back to that, once and for all."

Hollywood Darling Ivy Stone's Twin Sister Dead

March 31st, 2016

Hollywood is shocked and reeling this morning about the death of Ivy Stone's twin sister. Camilla was Ivy's assistant and had joined Ivy on location in Cold, Montana a few weeks into the filming of the upcoming movie *Cold*.

Sources say Camilla was jealous of Ivy and pretended to be her in an attempt to experience some of her stardom but, at the hands of a killer, paid the ultimate price.

Boyce Williams was a producer on the film and an integral part of the casting of Ivy for the role. Our sources say he started his obsession with the Hollywood starlet the day he met her.

"It was twisted," an anonymous source commented. "But he was insistent about having her in the film no matter what."

We don't know about you, but we think sometimes it pays *not* to know people.

STARS MAG ONLINE

Ivy Stone Hides Away Amidst Emotional Breakdown

April 3rd, 2016

Despite her return to Hollywood for the burial of her sister, no one has seen or heard from Ivy Stone.

Inside sources claim she's on the verge of a full-on mental breakdown. Screaming, breaking things, yelling at those closest to her. Apparently, she's really gone off the deep end.

We're wondering if this is the end of her career or if the crazy side of her will make her even more marketable.

We can't wait to find out!

CHAPTER ONE

Levi

April 4th, 2016

WARM WATER WASHED DOWN OUR BODIES AND MINGLED WITH Ivy's silent tears.

She'd been crying them for the entire twenty minutes we'd been under the spray, and I still didn't think she'd actually felt them.

Silent and stark, she was a shell of herself, and I was doing my best to make sure the thin exterior didn't break.

"Tilt your head back," I instructed softly, working my fingers through the tresses of her thick hair to rid it of the sudsy shampoo.

Extending her neck and letting the weight of her grief sink deeper into her shoulders, she complied.

There was no sign of contentment, no fire of contempt, and no relief in the warmth of the water or my gentle touch. She'd shut out everyone and everything the moment Dr. Ines had broken the news of Camilla's passing.

Police questioning, meeting Ivy's distraught parents, traveling to LA—it was all a blur.

For me *and* Ivy, I suspected.

Ivy was lost in her grief, and I was lost in being there for her.

On a normal basis, we try to live our lives looking outward. What's in front of us, what's around us, what's worthy of finding out more.

But now, my sole purpose was seeing to the well-being of the woman I loved. My view was focused inward. In the window. Inside the house. Away from the noise.

At the heart of Ivy.

Where she had a bottle of emotion just waiting to explode.

"Talk to me, baby," I urged. "Get it out."

Hard heart and blank eyes, she ignored my plea and my touch as I ran my hands down the slick skin of her shoulders and then back up to settle at her neck.

I tilted her chin with the pressure of my thumbs, bringing her defiant, distraught eyes to meet mine. She fought the contact, fully aware of intimacy's ability to tap into well-hidden emotion. She didn't want me breaking through the façade. She wanted it to hold strong—she wanted the distance to protect her.

I'd used the technique for years of my life, torturing myself and those around me, and I recognized the look of it in her.

I was hesitant to resist anything she felt she needed—but I *knew* better.

Self-contained grief only multiplied. It attacked its only available opponent and destroyed the person appropriately. I didn't want to watch her destroy who she was. Lively, fiery, and full of life. She had so much to offer, and I couldn't imagine her turning into a female version of what I'd been for so many years.

"Ivy," I called. "*Look* at me."

Deprived of her solitude, she lashed out, whipping my skin with the lash of her tongue. "Leave me alone."

"No," I refused. "I'd do just about anything you asked. But I won't do that."

"Get out!" she screamed, high-pitched and desperate, splashing the water against the thick marble tile as she slashed out an arm.

I wrapped my arms tightly around her body, trapping her arm beneath them, and pulled her close. "No," I repeated. "Not now, not ever. You and me against everything else. You and me, no matter the obstacle, we face it together."

The words were like a hammer to the wall she'd built. Brick by brick, she crumbled into my arms and gave herself over to the emotion.

"I just... How do I do it, Levi? How am I supposed to say goodbye?"

Squeezing my arms tighter, I put my lips to her hair and breathed in her pain. If I could take it from her and put it inside of myself, I would.

My voice shook as I tried to find the words to give advice I hadn't followed myself. I had been a one-man shitshow until Ivy had come along. It felt ironic to be trying to put the pieces of her back together when the glue was still drying on myself.

"However you can. For me, I couldn't let go. I couldn't move past anything, and I think you know that better than anyone."

A sob tore from her throat as she pressed her face farther into my throat.

"And for as messed up as I was before you, I don't think I was entirely wrong." God, how could I say this in a way that made sense?

"I don't think you say goodbye. I think you try to understand that, physically, she's gone. But her spirit, the parts of her you love, they never will be. She'll guide you. She'll teach you. Just like you found with Grace, someone else will find a lesson in Camilla and learn from her."

"I just don't know how to handle today. All those people..."

Today, she'd bury her sister.

Today, she'd say goodbye.

Today wasn't a day at all. It was a real-life version of hell.

In fact, I'd been dreading this day since I'd attended Dane Marx's funeral in Cold. That one had been hard. He had been a good guy. Full of life. Honest. Kind. And he hadn't deserved his fate. He hadn't deserved to be snuffed out of this world at the hands of an unhinged psychopath.

And now, he'd left behind a distraught mother and father and sister trying to figure out how to pick up the pieces.

Fuck, what a mess. What a fucking mess.

They say the majority of police officers never have to shoot their guns during their careers. Much less have to kill anyone.

Yet I'd somehow managed to have blood on my hands twice.

Both of my victims deserved their fate, that much I knew.

But *their* victims? They were innocent. They were tragically removed from this life for no other reason but evil, deranged motivations.

Visions of Dane and Camilla threatened to flash behind my eyes, but I pushed them away. I refused to go there. I refused to wallow in the terrifying memories.

Ivy needed my strength.

I pulled her face from my chest and moved her head out from under the water. I wanted her to hear me, to see me—to know I meant the words with every fiber of my being.

"You do whatever you need. Anything, Ivy. And you do it knowing I'll be there, right next to you, every single step of the way."

CHAPTER
TWO

Ivy

SWEET TULIPS AND FRAGRANT LILIES, THE SMELLS OF THE FUNERAL home closed in on me like a compactor. Everything felt tight—stifling—and the eerie, low hum of people just barely talking felt so wrong.

Camilla was young and full of life, and the fact that she was gone couldn't have been more obvious in this dusty pink room if they'd tried.

The carpet was well-worn and the subfloor squeaky, and pictures littered the antique tables around the perimeter of a room filled with ornate chairs. It was fancy and top-of-the-line, but not one feature of the converted old house reminded me of my sister.

"Oh, Ivy," my mother's friend Lorraine cooed in my ear as she wrapped her arms around me. "Your *twin*. I can't even imagine how alone you feel."

The words, meant to comfort, I was sure, did nothing but incite my anger.

My looks were a curse, and being a twin to Camilla was the sole reason she was gone.

It should have been me.

I swallowed past the thick emotion in my throat and blinked

away the tears that never seemed to go away. Lorraine kept talking, but I couldn't hear a fucking word she was saying. She seemed intent on making this hug last far longer than it needed to, and her old-lady perfume threatened to choke the oxygen out of my tight lungs.

Levi stepped forward from beside me, pulling the frail woman from our embrace and capturing her attention, and I breathed a sigh of relief.

He'd been doing this since the moment we'd arrived at the visitation service this morning—any time my emotions elevated past the baseline agony I knew as my new normal, he stepped in.

He smiled and fawned. He hugged and small-talked. He did everything short of transplanting his body in the place of mine to take the attention off of me—even if it went against everything that came naturally to him.

He wasn't chatty and he wasn't social and he didn't like to be touched by hundreds of strangers at a time, but he dove headfirst into it today—for *me*.

Unfortunately, the line was never-ending and the comments all the same. As soon as one well-meaning busybody stepped aside, another took his or her place. Not to mention, the low keen of my mother's wail hadn't stopped since the start of the receiving line of friends and family. It was suffering and agonized, and I felt bloody and beaten from the intensity of it. I didn't know how the fuck I was going to survive it through the end of the funeral and repast.

And the words that everyone kept saying to me—words I knew were said with love and care—grated. They were ridiculous and trite, and the fact that anyone thought there was even a possibility of being okay at this point was preposterous.

My sister had just died, for fuck's sake. *God.*

I had to take a gulp of air to stave off tears as I remembered the moment Levi told me she'd been pretending to be me. That she'd *died* saving *me*.

FOX

We'd just arrived in our hotel room in LA, and I hadn't stopped asking questions about how this could have happened—*why* it would have happened to *Camilla*—since our plane had taken off in Montana. Levi's face had been nearly lifeless as he'd clasped me gently at the tops of my arms and settled me into the cushion of the couch without explanation.

And there, down on his knees, with his heart in his throat, he'd explained it all to me.

He'd started off by letting me know he hadn't been hiding the details of Camilla's death from me, but he had been waiting for the right time to explain it all. Which, when it came to the tragic murder of my sister, there was no right time. It was all horrible fucking timing.

But he'd told me nonetheless.

How it had happened. What had been going on when he'd arrived on scene. My sister pretending to be me to protect me from Boyce. His struggle to get a shot as Boyce had taken her from me. How Boyce had thought he was taking *my* life.

How was I supposed to get over the guilt of that? The reality that if I'd just been awake, Camilla would still be alive?

"You okay?" Levi whispered, pressing the side of his body up against the side of mine. The physical contact felt good, the warmth of his muscular arm seeping into the cold numbness of my own.

"No," I said simply, clenching my teeth to fight the sting of tears as they pooled behind my nose.

I wasn't okay. I wasn't coping. And I *wasn't* ready to let Camilla go.

Levi's small smile was the very last thing I expected. A villain among the frowns and tears of everyone else.

Granted, it was far removed from happy, reeking more of relief than anything else, but I couldn't reason what place it had here.

I watched the blue swirl in the circular midnight pools of his eyes and basked in the strength of his fingers intertwined with mine. Even when the someone I was rallying to face was him, I flourished under his support.

"Are you *relieved* that I'm struggling?" I asked through gritted teeth. My volume was low, but Levi took our privacy a step further by leaning down to my ear to answer.

"No, baby," he assured. "I'm relieved you're able to admit it. That means I might be able to help. That your family might be able to help."

I moved back just slightly, enough to study his eyes, but the moment didn't last.

My mother's gulping sob cut through my chest and pulled me around to face the front.

Just to the left of my father, she was struggling to stand at the head of our line, her previously crisp black dress wrinkled at the edges from all of the physical contact.

Mary Murphy was in her arms, swallowed by a hug full of grief, and a ratty tissue poked out from my mom's hand at Mary's back. Mary was a stranger to my mother, but she was no stranger to my mother's pain, and the sight of her made me go weak at the knees.

No obligation, no pressure, she and Sam had made the trip from Cold all the way to LA, just to be here for us in our time of need. If I'd ever had any doubts at all that the Murphys were the kind of family you dreamed of holding a place in, they were completely gone now.

Levi noticed my stare, followed the line of it to Mary and Sam, and reached out to squeeze my hand. Despite my short temper with him and everyone else, I took it in my own and clutched it so hard they might permanently join.

He nodded at me when I looked to him, a confirmation that the Murphys traveled here just for this. That I was important enough to them to show up, in my most desperate time of need.

As the familiarity of what she and Sam and Levi had been through over six long years ago pierced my chest, my hand tightened even further in its clutch of Levi's. He squeezed back and leaned down to kiss my cheek before leaving me to my moment.

I watched raptly as Mary took my mom's weight and whispered kind words into her ear. For the first time in the service, I found myself eager for the line to move faster—eager to talk and hug and thank someone for coming.

She knew exactly what my family was feeling. Grace was her daughter, and one minute her baby girl, her child, had been on this earth, vibrant and full of life, and the next she'd been gone.

Mary *knew*. She knew with an intensity that comforted and soothed. That gave reason to my feelings and my pains and put a face to where I might be able to live one day.

Settled in my grief. In no way over it, but certainly to a place where coping was possible.

I listened intently as Mary finally moved on from my mom and introduced herself to my dad. He took her hand in a firm shake, throat tight, but he didn't pull her into the bone-crushing hug my mother had.

My dad, Dave, was a totally trustworthy guy. Dependable. Funny in the dad-joke kind of way and strong. He was always there for his girls.

But in the face of losing one, he was nothing more than taciturn. Short nods. Small words. He couldn't bear the thought of giving any of these people any more of himself than a polite greeting.

I didn't blame him at all.

Where my mom found comfort in crying into nearly anyone's arms, my dad and I held ourselves removed.

But as Mary stepped over to me and pulled me gently into her arms, I went without reservation. Her hug was warm and solid, and the sweet smell of her wrapped around me only served as a reminder of just how unfair the world was as a whole.

Deep breath expelled, I couldn't stop the sob that followed as I opened my throat and leaned into the embrace.

"You're doing so well, Ivy," Mary murmured into my hair. I nodded into her neck, flourishing under the praise. I didn't know why it helped so much, but somehow, thinking she was satisfied with the way I was handling everything made me feel validated. If she thought I was starting where I needed to, maybe I'd be able to get to where she was.

"I…" I choked on saliva and started over. "I just can't believe this happened."

Mary stroked my hair and hummed softly before responding. "That never goes away. The why, the how, it'll plague you forever. But by God, the rest of it will get easier. Give yourself time. Give yourself grief. Give yourself whatever it is you need, and lean on those around you."

I nodded as she pulled back from the hug and tipped her head toward Levi. "Really," she emphasized. "He's tall and strong, and he can handle your load. Give it to him."

"Okay," I whispered softly.

A gasp sounded from behind me as Sam shoved Mary out of the way and embraced me heartily. The other attendees were taken by surprise by his frankness, obviously, but I was relieved. In fact, a tiny laugh formed in my throat and almost made it to the surface.

A miracle.

"Sam," I murmured affectionately as he squeezed me tightly. "Thank you so much for coming."

"When you get to be my age, funerals are about all you get to do outside of the house."

I shook my head at his obvious joke and placed a small kiss on his cheek. The warmth of his smile took root inside my chest and bloomed as he basked in it.

"Thanks anyway," I told him again. "I'm so glad you're here. Please come eat with us after. To the repast. Levi can give you directions."

He nodded once and slapped Levi and me both on the arms. "Wouldn't miss it, doll. Like it or not, you're family now. To us. To Cold. And family looks out for family."

Truer words had never been spoken. My sister had certainly looked out for me.

CHAPTER
THREE

Levi

ITH A MIND TO IVY'S QUICKLY DRAINING ENERGY, I SCOOPED
another helping of pasta alla vodka onto her plate and
then set the serving spoon back in its place.

She was turned, listening to her aunt as she talked to her mother, a blank, hollow kind of torture coloring her face gray.

It'd been a horrible day, to put it mildly. Eager to get everything over with and limit the amount of media attention, Helen, Dave, and Ivy had chosen to do everything—visitation, funeral, and repast—on the same day. I'd hired security for us, guys who used to work on the police force before moving into the private sector, and they'd done a great job of making sure I didn't have to worry about Ivy's safety.

I glanced their way, and the man in charge, Baylor, gave me a nod while his partner, Hampton, surveyed the room.

The decision to do it all in one day had been a good one, it seemed, for media. Word of the service hadn't gone public until a couple of hours in, and by then, the area had been fully secured and locked down.

But that didn't mean it didn't come with drawbacks. Ivy had been on her feet for the better part of eight hours, and emotionally, she was drained.

After a week of waiting to lay Cami to rest, and the reality of doing it, she was barely hanging on at all.

Carefully, I brushed the hair from her shoulder and leaned forward to put my lips to her ear.

"Eat, baby. Carbs are good."

She startled at the sound of my voice but didn't turn.

"I'm not hungry."

"I know," I conceded. My stomach knew the twisted, vacant illusion grief created. It said we didn't need sustenance when we did; that we didn't need the energy to go on. But now, on the other side of the cliff looking back, I knew better. The time would come when she'd need the fuel, when the energy would be welcome. And I wanted her to be ready. "Eat anyway."

For the rest of today, for tonight—she would need it. I knew she wouldn't be ready to rest until the very last tear had been shed, the last hug had been given, the memories had been basked in with her mother, and she'd already been going for so long.

Her glare was noticeable as she turned, but I took the fork in her hand as victory.

I needed her to eat. I didn't need her to like me while she was doing it.

When I turned away from her and back to my plate, leaving nothing but an arm at the back of her chair to keep closeness established, I found her dad watching me. His eyes were keen, shiny with emotion, and, most important of all, approving.

And I didn't need a decoder ring to know why.

The man's heart was heavy and riddled with holes, and the stress of looking out for both his wife and daughter was almost unmanageable.

I was willing to help carry the burden of his family. I was willing to wade through the misplaced guilt of survivors left behind. And he was relieved to have the assistance.

Sam caught my attention from the bar across the room with a wave of a hand, so I leaned to the side and placed a kiss to the apple of Ivy's cheek. She flinched at the contact.

"I'll be right back," I told her. "Just going to get a refill and say hello to Sam. Can I get you anything?"

She shook her head but said nothing, likely still mad about the food. I kissed her again and ignored the glare before rising out of my chair and stepping the two feet over to her dad. "Can I get you anything while I'm up, Dave?" I asked.

He startled at my question and looked up to find my eyes. Deep hazel and searching, his own were struggling to place me, even having made direct mental contact with me moments before. The grief-stricken mind was a bottomless ocean of confusion. Facts flitted and details roamed, and nailing down any one feeling was an impossibility—blocked off in an exercise in self-preservation.

"What's that?" he asked in a fog.

I smiled kindly and repeated the question. "I'm headed over to the bar. Can I get you or Helen anything?"

"Uh, no," he stuttered. "I think I'll head that way myself in a minute. Could use the breather."

I nodded my acquiescence and moved away, happy to give him the moment he needed to gather himself. I hated having people in my face, especially people I didn't know well, when I was doing my best to process unwelcome emotion.

I glanced to Baylor and jerked my head, assuring he would keep an extra eye on Ivy while I was talking to Sam.

Baylor was an expert in his field, and a guy cut from my own professional cloth. He nodded back and signaled to Hampton that he'd be stepping farther into the room.

I exhaled a breath of relief and moved swiftly to the bar.

Sam was downing a glass of whiskey like a man half his age.

I smiled and nudged him with my shoulder as I sidled up next to him. "Needed a drink, huh?"

Sam guffawed. "Just about always anymore, Lee. But today, yeah. Especially today."

Emotions raged on the surface as he relived the death of his own granddaughter. I could see it written in the tense line of his shoulders and the hard line of his jaw.

"Stirring up some shitty stuff," I murmured, nodding to the bartender to get me a glass just like it.

Unlike the times of the past, I wouldn't be overindulging today. I just wanted a little sip to take the very edge off.

Sam nodded and licked his lips, admitting, "It's hard. Doesn't ever stop being hard, and I know you know exactly what I mean. And poor Ivy. I feel for that girl like she's one of my own. I wish I could say I can't imagine the guilt she's carryin' around, but you and I both know we've seen it before."

Me. He was talking about me, and the guilt I'd carried for years after Grace's death. My throat tightened and my palms flexed, and all I could do was nod.

"How you holdin' up?"

I shrugged. Who the fuck cared how I felt? To me, all that mattered was Ivy.

Sam shook his head and smacked me on the hand like a nun scolding a student. I pulled my hand back and rubbed it with a laugh. "What the hell was that for?"

"For being an ass. You gotta take care of yourself to take good care of her. Number one goddamn rule. Don't be a jackass and fuck it all up by going into a tailspin of your own."

I smiled at his frank words and gave his shoulder a thankful squeeze. Sam had always been like a grandfather to me, and I didn't know what I'd do when I didn't have him to turn to one day.

"I hear you. I promise. But I'm okay, Sam. All the shit. Everything I saw, everything I've been through. She's alive, and she's mine. I'm not going to do any-fucking-thing to mess that up."

My eyes followed my thoughts, straight across the room to the woman of my dreams. Ivy had finished the pasta on her plate and had found a comforting spot in the crook of her dad's arm. She was a vision, even cuddled up and reflective. Her soft face, her active green eyes. All of it just pointed to the fierce spirit inside of her I really loved.

Of all the places I never thought I'd go, Hollywood was it.

But seeing her with her dad and knowing the horrific grief of her mom, I had a feeling I was going to have to get used to it.

For as long as Ivy needed her parents, and for as long as they needed her, we'd be here to stay.

Everything else could wait.

My job on the force.

My life in Cold.

Everything.

I felt like a bit of a bastard for even having the luxury of a hefty inheritance to fall back on, but I guessed, ironically, it was the one time I could actually feel grateful toward my late father.

But it was my reality, and for once, I really was thankful.

The day before we flew out of Montana, I'd let the chief know I'd be taking a leave of absence. I had no idea when or if I'd be back, and honestly, it was of zero importance to me.

Ivy was my focus.

I needed her, and she sure as fuck needed me.

CHAPTER
FOUR

Ivy

April 11th, 2016

CHOKING FEAR CLOGGED MY AIRWAY AND MADE IT HARD TO breathe as Boyce wrapped his arm around my throat and put the blade of the knife against my skin.

A little droplet of blood trickled and tickled at my neck, and the first real visions of actual death washed over me.

There was a chance—a horrible, unfathomable chance—that I wouldn't make it out of this alive.

The only thing grounding me to the moment was the thought of my sister, sleeping soundly in the back room.

She was an innocent bystander, a secondary character on the path of my life that had led us to here. All I needed—all I wanted—was to keep the focus on me and keep it off of her.

"Boyce," I whispered, breathing shallowly. "Why are you doing this? I don't...I don't understand."

His laugh was maniacal and otherworldly as he sliced the blade across my throat without an answer.

The bed rocked as I sat up abruptly, my breathing erratic and panicked, a silent scream disturbing the air as it tried to make it into my lungs.

My chest thudded wildly, and my eyes scoured the room for something, anything to make me feel better. Unfamiliar linens tickled at my fingertips as my eyes tried to adjust to the overwhelming darkness of the room and bring my heart back to a normal pace.

I wasn't in the small house I'd rented while filming in Cold, Montana, and I certainly hadn't been the one under the torturous strain of Boyce's knife.

The soft sounds of a city teased outside and helped it all come rushing back to me.

Levi and I were at the Beverly Wilshire in Beverly Hills, and we'd been here for the last week and change. Camilla's burial had come and gone, and all that was left was me, Levi, a hotel room, and a bottomless well of unresolved questions.

All at once, the agony rushed back, crushing and debilitating to the point that it felt like the actual blade I'd dreamed of.

I could feel the metal at her throat and the fear in her chest, and I ached to make it go away.

I needed air.

I needed answers.

I needed *Camilla*.

Oh God.

Why? Why did this have to happen to her? My sister. My twin. My best fucking friend in the whole wide world.

My skin itched and my legs danced under the blanket as I tried to calm the race of my heart. I wanted to rewrite history, turn it on its head and relive the night just as I'd dreamed it.

I didn't want to die, but I would have given anything to do it if it meant I could take my sister's place.

Levi's breathing elevated as I thrashed back and forth next to him, and when I looked at his handsome face, it all became too much.

The history. The horrible way I'd treated my sister because of emotional avoidance when it came to how I'd felt about him.

I wanted a do-over. For *all* of it.

Swiftly, I threw the covers off my legs and jumped from the bed. The room was dark and relatively quiet, and the blackout curtains were meant to keep it that way.

For now, I didn't mind, eager to escape myself and the feelings crawling under my skin.

Uncertainty was a horrible mask for grief, but it was the only thing I had to work with to occupy the hours. The more questions I asked, the more work I had to do to search for answers, and the busier it would keep me while I waited for the knife of reality to stop twisting.

Our hotel room was a suite, something Levi had insisted on so that security could be with us at all times. There were two bedrooms on the other side of the common living room area where they were staying and a small kitchenette by the entrance. We hadn't actually used the kitchen at all, but the space had been nice long term.

The irony of having a house here that I wasn't using wasn't lost on me, but I'd shared that home with Camilla. I couldn't even think about going back.

Not wanting to wake anyone else, I left the door to our bedroom shut and moved to the walk-through closet that led to the bathroom. In there, I could turn on the lights, splash my face with water—try to breathe again.

I closed the door behind me with a quiet click before flicking on the light, and I rested my palms against the marble of the vanity top.

Each breath felt wracked and broken, and it took me a while to calm down enough to even turn on the water.

Focusing on the cold tap only, I turned the knob and pooled my hands under the stream to gather some water, and then bent to the sink and splashed the cool, wet relief across my eyes and cheeks.

It chilled my burning skin and soothed the raw ends of my nerves, so I soaked in it, keeping my eyes closed and letting the excess drip into the sink like a song.

Cam's playful laugh flitted in my mind as she scrubbed off my facial mask, avocado smear on her own in the most comical of self-made skin remedies. I could see her so vividly, no matter that the memory had been formed two years ago, and my chest squeezed.

She was the best sister I could have ever asked for, even when I wasn't the same to her. Most times, I was demanding and spoiled and, fuck, I'd spent a lot of time chasing success instead of memories. It had been two weeks since she'd passed, but so far, no amount of time was making it any easier.

My hair drifted forward and into the water, so I shoved it back behind my shoulders and stood up straight.

The fluorescent lights were harsh on the lines of my make-up-free, red-streaked face, and my wild hair stood out past my ears. But in the first moments of recognition, in the middle of a mass of red mane, all I could see was Camilla.

Staring at me. Begging me for help and wishing for absolution.

A sob clutched my throat and kept ahold of it as I struggled to get my anxiety under control.

"Your twin," I heard in my head. *"You look so much alike."*

Words from the funeral, words that'd been on repeat in my head, all of them swirled into an angry plague over my heart and threatened to stop its beating.

"Why?" I yelled at my reflection, a hard burst of despair overwhelming me. "Why did it have to be her?"

With her eyes staring back at me and the pain on her face, I lashed out at once, ramming my fist into the hard plane of the mirror and screaming.

For her. For me.

For Grace. For Levi.

FOX

For anyone who'd ever been through the torture I felt right then.

With a splintering web, the glass of the reflection shattered, and I cried out into the otherwise silent night as I fell to my knees.

My heart was battered and broken; I might as well have the hand to match.

CHAPTER
FIVE

Levi

THE JAGGED, PIERCING SOUND OF SOMETHING BREAKING WOKE ME from a dead sleep.

Startled, I reached out to feel for Ivy, to lay a hand on her to settle her nerves. I didn't know what had made the noise, but it was the very reason I'd wanted to have security close by at all times.

The bed beside me was empty, and with a brief sweep of my hand, I found the sheets were cool to the touch.

Ivy had been missing for a while.

Panic oozed, suffusing the sinew of my muscles and putting them on alert immediately.

My back cracked as I jumped up from reclining to standing in one swift motion, but I ignored the twinge in my spine and set out searching.

I'd meant to sleep with an ear to Ivy, but the stretch of days, two weeks and counting at this point, of avid attention had apparently rendered night watch impossible.

"Ivy?" I called into the darkness.

She didn't answer.

But a soft cry from the bathroom was all the indication I needed.

I moved expeditiously, rounding the bed in the nearly blacked-out

room and pulling open the curtains at the foot of it. The light from the full moon poured in and eased my way through the giant walk-in dressing room and into the bathroom, allowing me to move faster.

The door was closed but unlocked and swung in easily as I turned the knob.

Perched on the edge of the tub, Ivy was cradling a bloody hand and crying quietly.

"Ivy," I murmured, the whisper of my voice tortured with the knowledge of what had driven her to this point. Pain, acute and all-consuming, made you feel like anything would relieve the itch to crawl outside of your skin. Even physical harm.

"What happened?" I asked, glancing to the shattered mirror before rephrasing my question to the more important one. "Why did you do this?"

"I can't stand it," she declared in an aching whisper. Tears carved rivers down her cheeks, and the slice of her voice cut me up inside.

My chest tightened exponentially.

"Seeing her everywhere I look. Half the people at the funeral commented on how we were...how I'm..." A sob broke from her throat. "No matter what I do, I can't stop myself from seeing her when I look in the mirror. I can't stop myself from seeing myself in her place and wishing that's the way it was."

God.

Blood trickled down her bare leg and pooled on the floor as she squeezed at her injured hand with the other.

The physical pain was an escape—a shift of focus—but it certainly wasn't healthy. I couldn't sit aside and watch her torture herself just because she wanted to take Cam's place. I understood her drive, but fuck, the mere thought of that reality felt like a cleaver to the heart. I didn't know where I'd be if Ivy had been the one at the edge of Boyce's blade.

"Baby, stop," I ordered softly, forcing her hands to separate with

a delicate tug of her wrist. "Let me look at this."

"No!" she yelled, yanking the carnage back from me. "You have to do something. You have to make it so I don't see her in the mirror anymore!"

"Ivy—"

"You have to!" she bellowed.

A knock on the door brought my head around as Baylor called through the door, "Everything all right?"

The screaming had apparently finally awoken the other people in the hotel suite.

"Yes," I called back swiftly, knowing Ivy would want privacy. Baylor was a trusted employee, and I knew he wouldn't spread any of what he saw behind closed doors around to the media. He'd done a great job of seeing to our privacy for the last two weeks, and for the time we'd been in LA, he'd even sent Hampton to run most of our errands.

Sure, being in the room all the time was a little bit stifling, but I knew Ivy wasn't ready to have the eyes of the world upon her. Hell, six years after Grace's death, I wasn't ready for one set of fucking eyes. Even brilliant, loving green ones. I couldn't even imagine millions of judgmental ones.

"No," Ivy called suddenly, defying me. My eyebrows pulled together as I surveyed her face, but she was determined. "I need a box of hair dye," she called through the door. "Blond."

"Ivy," I murmured, knowing the decision to home-dye her hair a completely different color wasn't the kind of thing you did in the middle of the night. It wasn't the kind of thing you didn't carefully pick out yourself, and you didn't do it in a hotel bathroom unless you were on the run from the police.

"Blond?" Baylor called to confirm.

"Ivy," I said again, trying to intercede.

"No, Levi," she protested, shoving me away and getting to her

feet. "I'm doing this. With or without your help and I'm doing it now."

"Let me look at your hand, Ivy," I ordered, a gravelly need making my throat roll.

"If you dye my hair, I'll let you look at my hand." Her face was hard and determined, and I knew I didn't have any wiggle room at all.

She'd said it herself; with or without me, she would be doing this, and she would be doing it now. But with me, I could look after her. I could do the work so that she could keep a bandage on her hand.

"Baylor," I called, closing my eyes and taking a deep breath as I dropped my head forward. "Blond dye. Bandages. And a first aid kit. Please."

His response was immediate, and so was my regret. "Yes, sir."

Still, there was no turning back now.

■

I closed the door behind me, CVS bag in hand, and Ivy shifted from her perch on top of the toilet.

While we had waited for Baylor to get back, I'd convinced her to hang her hand over the edge of the sink and let me check it for pieces of glass.

Luckily, she'd listened to *those* instructions.

Everything else, though? Not so much.

She'd been a terrible patient, grouchy and uncooperative and completely resistant to everything I suggested. But she was talking to me, and after a battle, she eventually gave in.

For as difficult as I had been to manage for the last six years, I thought she was doing swimmingly.

"Hand first," I decreed, capturing Ivy's glare and absorbing it without resistance. I was all about making my woman happy, but I'd be damned if I was going to delay any longer in seeing to her well-being.

"Come on and stand up, baby," I ordered gently. "I need to wash it out."

She moved without much of a fuss and stood, facing the sink and standing in front of me. I reached around her body, enveloping her with my own and heating the surface of her back with the touch of my chest. She shivered at the contact.

We'd been *together* since Camilla's passing, but it hadn't been without its weirdness. She was either stiff or way too aggressive, and she had a really hard time closing her mind down enough to enjoy herself. I was more than willing to wait for her to get back to herself, but she'd been insistent each time we'd had sex. Still, I was always careful to let her lead, just to be certain she didn't feel pressured.

Carefully, I pulled the skin of her hand this way and that, searching a final time for slivers and gently washing out the cuts. Her knuckles had suffered the worst of it, but overall, it seemed like she'd gotten pretty lucky.

"This doesn't look too bad," I told her, washing each finger free of the stains from dried blood. "I think it should heal without too much scarring."

She laughed humorlessly. "Well, that's good. I guess at least some part of me should get out unscathed."

Deeply and affectionately, I sighed and shoved my lips into the hollow between her chin and collarbone. She smelled like the woman I knew, but the words said something else.

It'd be a long time before she healed completely.

Silent and thinking, we both went through the rest of the motions without comment. She was lost in her head, and I was trying to let her be. Feelings were meant to be felt, and it seemed wrong to deny her any outlet that didn't end with her cutting up her hand.

The directions to the dye were fairly simple, so I set out on my task while she stared at the wall.

It wasn't changing, and maybe that was its appeal.

But knowing something else wouldn't change prompted me to remind her. To tell her so she knew and always would, that no matter the circumstances, she and I would be in this fight together.

"I love you, Ivy. Red hair, blond hair, no hair, I love you."

Her eyes closed slowly, and her chin lifted to me. With her lips upturned and her face serene, I took the opportunity and robbed her of space.

Flesh to flesh, lips to lips, everything else melted away.

When I pulled back several moments later, she only had one thing to say.

"I love you too, Levi."

CHAPTER
SIX

Ivy

THE NEXT DAY, BAYLOR AND HAMPTON FLANKED MY SIDES AS WE
snuck into the hair salon through the alleyway door.

The front was busy, so no one other than those who
knew we were coming noticed our arrival. The owner of Salon
Vishon, a woman who'd identified herself as Holla on the phone
when Levi had contacted her, ushered me down a short hallway quietly and with a large smile, and she ducked into the back office set up
with a makeshift salon chair and wash sink.

"Okay," she said. "I hope this is okay. Everything in the front is
very open space—I was going for a modern feel—so I figured you'd
be more comfortable back here."

I nodded and scanned the small space. There weren't any windows, and there was a stack of folded towels waiting to be put away
in the corner, but overall, it was tidy and organized. It would be the
perfect place to keep anyone on the outside from knowing I was in
here.

"Okay, then," she said when I didn't say anything. "Take a minute to get settled, and Brina will be in shortly. She's been fully briefed
on the situation and knows to keep this close to her vest."

The discretion wasn't exactly new—I'd been a celebrity for a while—but Camilla's death took it to a whole different level.

This was about more than simple privacy.

This was about protecting myself from the world and the world from me.

As much as people thought they wanted a glimpse of me at my lowest, I could assure them they would regret it.

I knew.

I'd been looking at myself in the mirror for the past two weeks— since Camilla's death—and last night, I'd finally broken.

"Thanks," I murmured softly, glancing to my security as Holla stepped out the door.

They were huge guys, both over six feet and pushing two hundred and fifty pounds of solid muscle each. It was obvious they trained not only to keep their physique looking good, but to make sure it worked for them when they needed it to.

They kept to themselves, though, a trait I appreciated given the current state of my mind. I wasn't fishing for small talk or compliments, and I didn't have it in me to ask anyone about their families, significant others, or personal goals.

"We'll be right outside the door if you need anything," Baylor murmured, seemingly sensing my need to be alone. I nodded as he did one last survey of the room and then followed Hampton out and left me to my peace.

The stylist had yet to make her way back here from the front of the salon, and I didn't care why. The quiet moment was welcome, and I used the time to remove the baseball cap from my head.

Knowing Levi would be worried, I dug my phone out of my purse, dumped the cumbersome bag on the counter, and sent him a text. I ignored the forty missed calls from Mariah, Jason, and everyone else. I hadn't seen them since their brief drop-in at the funeral, and I didn't have any desire to change that anytime soon. I couldn't even think about work or acting or anything to do with something as trivial as normal, everyday life.

Reserved and to the point, I set out to put Levi's mind at ease, but I didn't give him much else.

Me: *I'm here.*

Levi: *Good. I'm glad you agreed to go.*

Like there'd been an option. I'd taken one look at the mess he'd made of me and known instantly that some things were better left to the professionals, no matter how much you didn't want to visit them.

Me: *Well, you pretty much mutilated my hair. I didn't have much choice.*

Levi: *Well, you pretty much mutilated your hand and refused treatment until I did your hair. You only have yourself to blame.*

I caught myself just before the corner of my mouth could curve up. A hint of happiness, a glimpse into the past. The crushing blow of reality was almost soul-destroying.

I wasn't ready to smile.

I didn't *deserve* to smile.

Me: *Do you have to make jokes?*

I cringed at my own bitchiness once I saw the text delivered inside our message box.

It seemed taking things out on Levi was my new MO. Rage, tears, inconsolable mumbling, he dealt with all of it.

And he'd been unflappable. An honest to God rock in the face of my turmoil. But I still found fault in nearly everything he did and everything he didn't. It wasn't about him, obviously, but that didn't make my treatment any more pleasant.

I worried he might tire of having to take my beatings, but he'd yet to show any signs of fatigue.

God, I hoped and silently prayed it wouldn't come to that. As much as I criticized and argued, Levi Fox was the only thing holding me together right now.

I needed him more than I needed oxygen...or this stylist to fix my god-awful hair.

Levi: Yes. Because as sad as it was that you were that desperate, the green vomit color of your hair right now makes it necessary.

Me: I'm not ready for jokes.

Levi: I know. But you will be one day. And I'll be here, ready to make them when you are.

A knock on the door sounded as I put my phone away without answering.

I knew it wasn't exactly the right thing to do, ignoring him rather than recognizing the sheer effort he was putting into being a foundation strong enough to hold me together, but I didn't have the energy to argue.

He could see the light at the end of the tunnel, and I was trying to do the same—honestly. It was just that the more I searched for the beaconing light, the more the walls seemed to be closing in. I wasn't ready to be done being sad. I wasn't ready to be done being mad.

"Yes?"

Baylor pushed open the door just enough to lean his head in.

"Ready?"

I nodded despite the nerves fluttering inside my stomach and settled into the black leather of the salon chair in the center of the room.

A petite blond woman slid inside, and Baylor shut the door behind her. She looked even more nervous than I felt.

"Hi," I whispered, trying to calm her down. There was only room for one basket case in here, and I'd sure as hell called dibs.

She squeaked.

"You know who I am?" I asked slowly—patiently, even. I was pretty impressed given my lack of impulse control these days.

She nodded, the bob of her head making her hair shake. It was big and wavy, but styled impeccably. I hoped like hell I'd come out of here looking a little closer to her.

Because right now, I was a disaster. Levi's characterization of my hair as the color of green vomit wasn't without basis. It was like a moldy blob on my head, and I wasn't sure I'd ever be able to get the green hue all the way out.

The only thing I did know—the only thing that made it a little easier to breathe—was that it wasn't red.

Eager to soothe the poor girl's nerves, I stuck out a hand and introduced myself anyway. She might have known who I was, but introductions went a long way in opening the gates of communication. If I gave her my name, she had to give me hers and so on.

"I'm Ivy."

She gulped but managed a hand in my direction and a soft breath of words. "I'm Brina."

"Nice to meet you, Brina."

I tried to lighten the tone of my voice. To save this stranger from having to carry the burden of my grief. "As you can see, my hair kind of had an incident."

She giggled and nodded. "Yeah. It looks a little abused."

I smiled as the ice between us started to crack. "Yeah. Well. I'm hoping you can make it look a little less like swamp thing and a little more like yours. Is that possible?"

Finally engaged in something in which she excelled, Brina dropped the timidity and stepped forward to pull the ponytail holder from my hair. As it cascaded over my shoulders, she oohed. "You have awesome hair."

I warmed a little. "Thank you."

"The good news is that it doesn't look like you did too much damage. The worst part is your roots—I'm a little afraid to strip any more color from them. I don't want to damage your hair permanently or burn your scalp."

I nodded my understanding and bit my lip, wondering what she would do if treating that wasn't an option.

"I think what we can do is just give you a dark, rooty look, instead of taking the blond all the way to the scalp. It's really in right now, so it shouldn't cause any problems for you work-wise."

I winced at the thought of going back to work. I truly didn't know if I'd be able to do it anymore. All I really wanted at this point was to be alone.

Alone with Levi, anyway.

"I'm not that concerned about work," I told her. "Just wanting it to be different. And somewhat normal."

"You should be perfect, then," she assured.

I didn't know about perfect—even the thought was horrendously abstract at this point—but at least there'd be one thing under my control.

And I really liked the idea of that.

■

Color applied, foils installed, I was sitting under the dryer they'd wheeled in while I processed and flipping through a gossip magazine.

An article a third of the way in was talking about me, and like some kind of sadist, I hadn't been able to stop myself from reading it.

Camilla's name was a fleeting mention as they focused on me and what this would do to my mental health. One "source" speculated that I wasn't that close with my sister and would be sure to recover quickly, while another predicted I'd be the next big celebrity breakdown. All of it was ridiculous and unfounded, and I wondered where on earth they found their material.

A commotion outside the door started up just as I tossed the magazine aside, and Baylor's voice rose authoritatively.

Instinct taking over, my heart pulsed with fear. Even knowing I had two large, fully capable men outside looking out for me, I still flashed through the possibilities of someone else getting to me.

I jumped as the door opened, but it was just Baylor. He looked stern and unyielding as he asked me what I wanted to do. "There's someone here to see you, Ivy. Says she's your publicist."

I swallowed hard around the lump in my throat and rubbed at it with a nervous hand. "Is her name Mariah?"

"Yes, ma'am. I noticed her at the service a week ago."

I nodded, not really wanting to see anyone I worked with, but knowing it would just cause more of a scene if I refused her now.

Mariah shoved in the door, glaring attitude over her shoulder at Baylor as she did. When she got a look at me, though, all the fire died.

I could only imagine the state of my face. I hadn't worn makeup since the funeral, and my sleep had been lacking, to say the least.

My cheeks felt cold and hollow, and my skin sagged with my misery.

"Oh, honey," Mariah said, heartfelt and familiar. I didn't expect it at all, especially not to like it, but it was good to see her.

She rushed forward as I opened my arms, and she fell into my hug. I fought hard against dissolving into tears. Lately, I had quite the problem with turning off the tap once they started flowing.

"God, Ivy," she whispered near my ear. "I know I said all of this to you at the funeral, but I just can't stop thinking about everything and I'm just...I'm so, so sorry about Cam. And that you had to go through all that. I had no idea about Boyce."

The sound of his name so close to my ear was like a shot to the heart, and I pulled away. I didn't want to have trust issues, but the fact was, I did. And she'd just reminded me that she'd been the one to get the meeting for my original casting call.

"About that," I started as she pushed back to her feet and looked down to me earnestly. "You got me the meeting with him. It's one of your biggest bragging claims to fame, Mariah."

She was shaking her head before I could even finish, so I pushed on.

"No. I'm sorry to be like this, but I have to know why. What made you push for the meeting?"

She swallowed and turned to the door before turning back. Her face was sallow with guilt. "Okay, so...I didn't. He called me, Ivy. Said you were just what they were looking for, and since he knew me, had been in touch with me before, he decided to go through me instead of Jason. I know I shouldn't have taken credit for getting you a meeting that fell into my lap, but—"

"You're saying you didn't suggest it to him?"

"No," she admitted softly and avoided my eyes. "He must have had his eye on you for a while."

I swallowed at the pain of the truth. I really had been the driving factor behind my sister's death. My actions had paved the way.

Mariah's voice was soft as she asked, "Have they made any connections between your stalker and this?"

I nodded around a lump in my throat. In hindsight, it'd been pretty obvious. Boyce had been the one stalking me the entire time, and the other celebrities he'd been stalking had all worked with him on previous films. I'd just been the only one to anger him past the point of no return.

"Listen, Ivy," Mariah murmured. "I know you need some time. So I'll stop calling for now. You let me know when you're ready, and we'll talk press junkets and other shit then."

My eyebrows drew together quickly.

"Press junkets?"

Mariah nodded. "For *Cold*. There's still a good year or more before it comes out, but they're wanting to schedule things now."

My mind swam as she kept talking.

"Anyway, I found out you were here and wanted to check in, but I'll tell everyone to wait. They can't do much without the star of the movie anyway."

The shake of my head was animalistic as I processed her words. "The movie…" I worked hard to breathe. "How can the movie still be happening?"

"What do you mean, sweetie? Why wouldn't it be?"

"*Why wouldn't it be?*" I gritted out, the pressure of my anger rising in my throat akin to thick bile. It was tangy and unwelcome, and I couldn't fucking control it. "My sister is dead!" I yelled, startling us both with the sheer volume of my shout. She took a step back toward the door, but it opened, and Baylor was striding in before she could get any farther than that.

"My sister is dead, and you people still care about a fucking movie!"

Mariah grimaced. "I-I'm so sorry, Ivy. I—"

"I really need you to go." I shut my eyes tightly. It was all too fucking much. "I just need you to leave."

I couldn't talk to her. I couldn't even look at her face.

How could they move forward with that fucking movie after everything that had happened? I mean, one of the fucking producers was the sole reason I'd had to bury my sister two weeks ago.

FOX

Before she could try to interject, Baylor pushed Mariah out, and Hampton finished the job while Brina and Holla rushed in with a cup of water and cookies.

I fought hard against lashing out again, but my chest wouldn't stop pulsing.

The news had been delivered, and it couldn't be taken back.

Some things happened; often, whether you wanted them to or not.

CHAPTER
SEVEN

Levi

"—IS STILL HAPPENING!" IVY YELLED, ONLY PROJECTING THE LAST HALF of her statement as the door slammed behind her so violently the room shook a little.

I could only imagine what the hell had happened since she'd left to get her hair done just four hours ago. Security had been with her the whole time, and I'd even checked in halfway through the process to make sure all was going well.

"What?" I asked, standing up from my spot on the couch. Her laptop was on the coffee table in front of me, and I'd been drafting an email to Jeremy.

He'd called and texted several times too, but Ivy and I had agreed not to get into any real details right now about timing or plans with anyone—even best friends.

We didn't have a strategy for our next move yet, and we wanted to make one together rather than being influenced by other people. Of course, that left my communication topics pretty sparse, and all I'd actually managed so far was a *Hey Jer, what's shakin'?* I imagined if Ivy's grand entrance hadn't interrupted me, I would have finished it off with an award-winning inquisition like *How are the girls?*

"What's going on?" I questioned, rounding the couch to take in

Ivy from head to toe. Her hair was greatly improved, even if the bags under her eyes were deepening by the day, and the spitting anger had put a little rose in her cheeks. All in all, she looked better than I'd seen her since the night everything happened.

With her showing no visible signs of injury, I'd have to rely on her storytelling ability to fill me in on the actual reasoning for her freak-out. These days, the cause could be nearly anything. "Are you okay?"

"No, I'm not okay! Mariah showed up!"

My brows drew together. "Where?"

"What do you mean, where?" she shouted with a stomp of her foot. "At the salon!"

My body instantly on alert, the line of my frame snapped straight and rigid. "How the hell did she know where you were?" And why the fuck hadn't security told me about it?

"Apparently, she tracked my phone," Ivy replied, tossing her hands in the air.

Any careful left in me fled with a vengeance.

"What the fuck?" I growled.

Ivy's sister had just been killed by a crazy stalker, and now her publicist was tracking her phone? No *fucking* way.

And how in the fuck was that even possible?

"I'm calling the cops." I rounded the couch again, headed back to the coffee table for my phone when Ivy stopped me with a tight grip around my bicep.

"No, no," she insisted quickly and with seriousness meant to get my attention. "I made that up. I don't know how she found me."

"For fuck's sake, Ivy," I snapped, losing my cool a little bit. "You can't just say shit like that."

It was slander at the very least and a whole fuckton of cans of worms at the worst. When it came to Ivy, I wasn't taking any fucking chances anymore, and any threat had to be treated with credibility on a large-scale level. One thing I'd never do again was trust her safety to just me. I was a trained professional, but quantity was important. I wanted several lines of defense all lined up in a row, and I'd be the last.

I made a mental note to have Baylor and Hampton start trying to figure out how the fuck Mariah had *actually* found her.

"Would you listen to the important part?" Ivy railed, throwing herself onto the couch and tossing her bag to the floor at the side. "Jesus!"

I clenched my jaw and reminded myself I'd pledged to let Ivy use me however she needed to feel better. And right now, she needed me to shut up and listen. It went against a whole lot of biological markers not to engage when someone argued with me, but for Ivy, I could find the self-control.

At least until she was back in fighting form.

"All right. What's the important part?"

"The movie! Mariah says it's in editing. They're going through with it."

I gentled my voice and kept her devastation in mind. I'd never thought they would shelve the project for fucking anything, but she'd obviously thought they would. "I suspected they would, baby."

"Why? Camilla was… That fucking psycho was a producer. They're still giving him credit!"

Logic and reason weren't exactly the best weapons in a talk with someone in the middle of a vent, but they were all I had to use. That, and my love. "Legally, they probably have to."

"Why on earth wouldn't they drop this thing? My sister died! You want to talk about legal? Where's the legal entanglement with that?"

"Baby," I started gently, advancing slowly to her place on the couch and dropping to my knees to take her face in my hands. "The studio has a lot of money wrapped up in this project. Contracts to fulfill."

"Who would even want to see it after all this?" Her voice shook with the evidence of vivid mental details. "Knowing what he fucking did to her?"

"A lot of people." The truth was, people were morbidly curious. Death and the events around it always attracted attention. If they didn't, the project never would have gotten to filming in the first place. "Truthfully, the studio likely knows the attention will bring in even more money."

Racked with disbelief and unwilling to accept it, Ivy jumped from the couch, her voice rising right along with her body. I moved enough to let her go but hovered close as she moved to the side of the couch and bent low to her bag, all the while yelling, "We have to do something! We can't let them do this!"

She dug her phone from her purse and started calling numbers. She glared as she waited, dropping the bag back to the floor and tripping on the strap as she started to pace. I jumped forward and freed her foot, and she kept walking like nothing had happened.

"Mariah!" she yelled into the phone when the ringing reached its culmination. She was a flurry of motion as she circled the room manically.

"Yeah, sorry for yelling at you before. I've got a lot on my mind."

A brief pause I wasn't convinced actually allowed for any talking on the other end observed, she dove right back in.

"Listen, I need you to get me a meeting."

She shook her head and snorted, but what she didn't do was cry.

She'd found purpose, apparently, in stopping the film from making it all the way to theaters.

I just hoped the fall wouldn't be too bad when the reality of almost certain disappointment set in.

"Yep," she confirmed. "Stan Feilding. Head of the studio. Just as soon as you can get it."

CHAPTER
EIGHT

Ivy

April 23rd, 2016

B AYLOR NODDED AS I STOOD UP AND BRACED MYSELF TO WALK into Stan Feilding's, the head of Trigate Films' studio, office.
His receptionist looked a little tired and a lot beaten by huge expectations, and I wondered how I'd fare in the room with the man who'd obviously spent most of his working hours making her look that way. Normally, I was a knowledgeable woman with vivid thought and clear expectations, but these days, my head seemed to be more of a mess than anything else.

Regret ached in my chest at having ordered Levi to let me go this alone, and it wasn't the first time. Since the funeral, I hadn't really let him go much of anywhere with me. We didn't do much outside of the hotel, but when I did, I'd been determined to go it alone.

I was so focused on being a professional—attending the meeting as an actress and a force to be taken seriously instead of a broken woman leaning on her boyfriend—that I'd forgotten the facts.

I *was* a broken woman leaning on my boyfriend, and my reasoning for asking the studio to reconsider moving forward with the movie was rooted in such. Causes were always better tackled by bigger numbers, and facing anything with Levi was better than facing it alone.

Somewhere along the way, I'd gotten lost in the floundering fight to be strong. But standing strong didn't mean you couldn't use the muscle of another person to do it.

And Levi had muscles in spades.

Still, I couldn't change my decision now. Mariah had spent a week and a half trying to get this meeting, and now that I was here, I couldn't just reschedule. I'd have nothing but the Levi in my head to hold me up and soothe me.

"Ah," Stan Feilding greeted as the door to his grandiose office swung open and his assistant ushered me inside. "Miss Ivy Stone. Come in, come in."

The space was large and intimidating, all black, red, and white décor. It was almost as though he'd taken a page directly from the *How to Appear Powerful* playbook.

"Hi, Mr. Feilding," I addressed him formally as I stepped cautiously into the room. My steps were slow but numerous as I closed the distance between us one foot at a time. "Thanks for agreeing to meet with me."

"Of course," he bellowed. "I like to make time for the people working within the company. And from your messages, it seemed to be important."

From halfway into the space, I stepped forward tentatively, and he gestured to the chair in front of his desk with a hand. "Please, take a seat."

My feet quavered as I did as offered and sank into the rich, red leather of his modern furnishings. He followed suit, tucking in behind an obnoxiously stately desk and smoothing his tie down his chest. His pepper-gray hair was perfectly coiffed, and his suit was neatly pressed. He was quite obviously a man with importance and money.

The thought struck me suddenly that what the two of us

qualified as important might not be on the same list at all. "Yes. Important to me, anyway."

He smiled a friendly smile, so I went on.

"My sister, Camilla—"

He was nodding before I even finished the sentence, and the unexpected motion caught me so off guard I stopped speaking. He obviously knew of her passing, as anyone with a pulse probably did, but something about his immediate confirmation made it all seem that much more real.

She was really, truly dead.

Sudden weight hit my chest, and pressure closed around my throat like a vise as I struggled to keep myself calm.

He filled the resulting void easily.

"Yes. I was deeply troubled by the news of your sister and one of my employees' role in all of it. I hope you know that the studio is willing to do whatever we can to make it right with you."

I was still recovering from the rush of reality, but his words brought air back to my lungs. They were positive. They were open. They were accommodating. My heart swelled slightly, inflated by sheer hope.

"Thank you, Mr. Feilding," I acknowledged. Having the head of a studio confront my need for a meeting with such human decency felt nice. Like maybe there was a little bit of right left in the world, after all. "I was really hoping you would say that."

Just one eyebrow arched, but his posture shifted more noticeably. In on his elbows, he leaned to the desk, but still somehow managed to make himself look taller.

"And what is it we can do for you, Ivy?"

I knew my request was a large one, but I had nothing to gain by stalling. "Not move forward with the project," I said simply. "With Boyce's involvement and the directly subsequent events—"

"Ivy, honey," he interrupted condescendingly. His tone was

sharp, and his face was completely different from before. His eyes weren't open and honest, and he wasn't humored by the ambitious nature of my wants at all. "Not moving forward isn't an option."

He didn't mince words, but the hope inside me still wouldn't die. I had to try. To see if maybe he'd somehow misunderstood me.

"Mr. Feilding—"

"It's in production. It's started the very expensive process of editing, and sound is already in development. We can't go back at this point, and I don't think you really want to," he said, taking it a step further by not only telling me his opinion, but pushing his off on me as a possibility. "Give yourself time to heal. You'll be ready by the time it comes out."

I frowned hard. His insinuation was insulting, to say the least. I was not a hysterical woman on a frivolous mission.

I was not a wounded heart dumped by some guy and hoping it would be better if I just erased the history on my browser.

I was a grieving sister and a respected employee of his company, and he wasn't actually giving me fucking anything. Despite what he'd made me believe at the beginning of the meeting. Despite what he'd surely tell the public happened if we got into a battle of truths.

"You just said the studio would do anything—"

"Not that, Miss Stone," he said with a finality that crushed my spirit and wounded my soul. "Anything," he qualified with a smile, "*but* that."

And just like that, everything I'd convinced myself I was going to change in myself went up in a puff of angry dust.

CHAPTER
NINE

Levi

THE DOOR SLAMMED, BUT THIS TIME, I DIDN'T STARTLE.

Anytime Ivy went out without me these days, it seemed she came back angry and itching for a fight.

Luckily, I was a bit of an expert in working out her aggression, and fighting was one of our most powerful love languages. To be honest, it'd been just about the only one she'd let me use lately to connect.

She didn't want my sweet words or soft offerings.

She wanted the battle. The brawn. The drag-out fight until all she could do to relieve the stress was take it out on my body.

Still, I hadn't given up hope that one day her feelings would change. That one day she'd long for my sweet embraces and soft touches, and she'd use them to heal her anger rather than fuel it.

I approached the door with open eyes and open arms, the way I started every encounter between us, and she smacked both down. "Don't," she said softly but curtly. "Just don't."

"Don't what?" I asked, using her own will against her. I would give her what she wanted but only for as long as she couldn't live without it. If she ever lost the will to tell me what I was doing wrong, I'd decided that would be my cue to tell me I was doing it right.

"Don't give your impassioned speech about calming down or relaxing or thinking it through," she told me easily, the steel in her voice all I needed to hear to take her seriously. Her throwing my words of the last week and a half right in my face wasn't a surprise. She'd tolerated it to a certain extent, but the meeting obviously hadn't gone her way, and she was done being a complacent listener.

She didn't want to be counseled or consoled. "I don't want to hear any of it."

I was well versed in the feeling. That didn't mean I couldn't push her, though. Challenge her wants. Test how close she was to giving in. My eyes slightly widened, I inclined my head.

"You want to fight?"

"I don't want to hear your bullshit soothing comments!" she shouted back, avoiding the question.

Oh yeah. She wanted a fight, even if she wouldn't ask for it. And if that was what she really needed, I was prepared to give her one.

"*My* bullshit?" I taunted. "*Your* bullshit, Ivy. Day after day, you oscillate between self-righteousness and self-destruction. You refuse to face the reality of the situation, and for all I know, you're going to be content to keep your head buried in the sand for the rest of your life. You want to see bullshit, look to yourself."

"I can't believe you'd say that to me. My sister is dead!"

"Yeah. She sacrificed herself for you. She gave her time and her patience to you when you needed it, she devoted her life to working for you. And then she loved you enough to protect you."

Ivy winced and then attacked. Her body slammed into mine and she raised a fist, but I caught her at the wrist.

"A fine showing you're making of that, huh?" I continued, pushing her to a dangerous edge, I knew. There was always a chance she'd leave me. That the facts I threw in her face would do the opposite of what was intended. That she'd build a wall I could never scale.

But the thought of not trying—of letting her go on like this for the rest of her life—was unthinkable. It was now or never. It'd been three and a half weeks since Camilla died, and if she wasn't willing to work with me now, I didn't think she'd ever be.

We were a team.

It was *together* that we could conquer anything. She just needed to be reminded of that.

"Stop," she yelled, tears bursting the dam and cascading down her cheeks. "You don't know anything!"

"I do!" I yelled back. "I *know*." Her face crumpled as the weight of my knowledge—my personal loss that she'd lived for months while making a film about it—settled over her. "I know how you're feeling, and I know the mistakes you're making in how you handle it. I know because I've been there."

"Levi, stop," she whispered, tortured. But something changed, I knew, because the distance was gone in an instant, replaced by the smell of her all around me and her face in my chest. Her hurt sank into me, and my knees buckled as I held on to support her. She gave it over to me and cried, changing the structure of her words to finally let me in. To finally look to me to help. "Just make it stop."

"I can't, baby," I admitted, the truth of which rocked me. Not being able to stop the thing hurting the woman you loved was akin to being hit repeatedly by a truck. Every time the crushing weight moved, it found you again, and the end was so far away it wasn't even in sight. But with her arms around me and her tears coating my shirt, I could sure as hell try to help carry the load. I could be there for her. I could love her. We could handle it together and create something that would honor the ones we'd lost. I told her the truth and she cried harder, but this time, they were tears of acceptance. "I can't stop it. I can only hold you while it goes."

All lips and tongues, our mouths danced together as we sought comfort in one another and stumbled back toward the couch.

Her hands were slower, less desperate than they had been in

weeks, and the feel of her touch as it lingered was almost like something new.

It was attentive and loving, and it spoke of a hope that the two of us would make it to the other side of this cloud.

Our relationship had been a lot of turmoil, but this was a turning of the tide. The waves were smoother and the emotion raw.

"I love you, Levi," Ivy said, her sweet declaration so welcome I couldn't even explain it.

She'd told me she loved me since Camilla died, but she hadn't done it with the intimacy that said she thought it meant something. The sincerity that thought it could survive.

Piece by piece, I stripped her of her clothes and reveled in her smooth, creamy skin. She was a goddess, and her green eyes glowed in the center of her much lighter hair. I was still getting used to the change, but she seemed at peace with it. I didn't care if she dyed her hair blue if it made it a little easier to get through the day.

Hell, she could've kept it green for all I cared.

I loved *her*. All of her.

"I love you too," I whispered, placing soft kisses down the bare line of her neck and settling at her chest. Her heart was beating a little faster than normal, but it was largely at ease. It didn't race with aggression or pound with fear.

It basked in the comfort of the two of us together.

"I don't know what I'd do without you," she murmured as her hands sank into my hair, and I latched my mouth on to her nipple.

Only at the height of her moan did I remove my mouth with a pop to answer her. "*You* healed *me*, baby. You brought me back from the brink."

She nodded, tears in her eyes. I undid my pants and pushed inside, bringing us together in the ultimate connection. It was everything I'd ever wanted, ever needed—she was those things.

She sighed, soft and content as I set a slow pace and brought my lips to hers. Silent but present, she held on with the grip of her legs and an intense wrap of her arms until both of us were drowning in the pleasure of our climax.

Only then did her mewl turn to words, and the set of them nearly broke my heart. "Can you heal me?"

So timid, so honest.

So mine.

"Yes," I vowed gruffly.

I would fight to the ends of the earth to make sure Ivy Stone healed from her wounds, and I'd destroy anyone who got in my way.

■

Quiet and reflective, we'd been lying on the couch, tangled in each other, for nearly half an hour when the next question finally made it past her lips. Her mind had clearly been running.

"What am I supposed to do?"

I didn't know what she meant, but I answered with the only thing relevant.

"You grieve. You do it how you need for as long as you need, and you lean on me."

"About the movie," she emphasized, a sort of broken thankfulness taking out the sting as she gave me a squeeze. "I can't believe they're going through with it."

Unfortunately, I could.

"The studio's top priority is making money, baby. I know this isn't what you want to hear, but it hasn't changed. No matter that you had better intentions, wanting to give the world a piece of Grace and a piece of the truth, money has been their motivator since the beginning."

"They have no moral compass."

"No," I agreed with a nod. "They never did, and they never will."

"Still. I can't just leave it at this, Levi. I just can't. I have to keep trying. For meetings with anyone who will listen. I have to try until I've been rejected by everyone."

Her tenacity was engrossing, and my heart swelled as she reasoned the possibility of disappointment on her own.

Chasing the studio with desperation to win was a disaster waiting to happen.

Chasing it for closure was the best thing she could do.

"Okay," I agreed. "You do what you have to do, and know that I plan to do it with you. We'll stay here for as long as you need."

Is Ivy Stone Spiraling out of Control?

May 1st, 2016

Despite attempts to keep herself out of the public eye since the death of her sister Camilla, Ivy Stone is still making the news. An inside source has revealed the Hollywood It girl has been keeping a low profile with her now-boyfriend Levi Fox in one of the luxurious suites at the Beverly Wilshire, but she hasn't been quiet.

Though her publicist has declined to comment on any and every question that has been sent to her office, a recent source has revealed that while Ivy is holed up at the Beverly Wilshire, she's been on an insane tirade to stop the movie Cold from being released to the public.

She met with studio heads to discuss her concerns, but apparently, the movie is still following its planned production path and will be released.
The current chaos surrounding Ivy Stone has us all wondering if there's more at play than just grief and sadness over the death of her sister.

Some skeptics have stated they believe alcohol and drugs could very well be a factor and are concerned Ivy will only continue to spiral toward rock bottom if she doesn't seek help.

Consider our ears to the ground as we wait for more updates on this ongoing Ivy Stone saga.

CHAPTER
TEN

Ivy

May 14th, 2016

A S WE PULLED INTO THE DRIVEWAY OF MY CHILDHOOD HOME, AN instant wave of tranquility washed over me.

Weeks of avoidance and battles had culminated last night, and Levi had finally taken the reins.

Reaching out to my mom and dad himself, he'd set the plans for today in motion, and against my wishes, had given me the exact thing I'd needed.

Stubborn me, I just hadn't realized it.

The comfort of my mom's sweet voice and the solace of my dad's bear hugs always made me feel better, no matter the hurt. They were the root of everything me and Camilla, and they were the reason I was the way I was. If anyone could tap into the antidote to my plague-like sadness, they were the ones.

Running from Camilla, her belongings, and our memories had seemed like the only answer to the pain. But I'd been trying that for a month and a half, and the days seemed to get slower and harder with each one that passed. Maybe the answer was in the opposite. In getting as close to her spirit as possible—in holding on tight to every part of her I still could.

I wanted to sit inside my childhood bedroom, and I wanted to lie down in Camilla's old twin-sized bed and just remember her.

Levi pulled the Range Rover to a stop and shut off the engine.

For as eager as I was to test the theory, I didn't hop right out. I stayed put in the passenger seat and let the emotions flow over me while I peered out through the windshield at my parent's midcentury modern home.

It was all clean, sleek lines and open, airy windows, and the entrance welcomed anyone who stood in front of it.

Home, I thought.

"You ready to go inside?" Levi asked, but I shook my head.

"I just need another minute." And I did. A moment to process, a moment to dread, a moment to accept that Cami wouldn't ever meet us at the door.

Patient with my ever-rocky emotions, he filled the silence by reaching out and clasping my fingers within his, resting our joined hands on the top of his thigh.

I felt so many things and all at once. It was damn near overwhelming, and I had to take a deep, shaky breath just to deal with it all.

Relief. Melancholy. Deep, soul-crushing sadness. And adrift.

So painfully lost.

I was about to walk into my parents' home, something I'd done a thousand times, but this time, I knew it wouldn't feel the same. It wouldn't give me an instant sense of comfort or relief.

I'd have to walk through the front door and face the memories of Camilla and me racing each other from the school bus to the house.

I'd have to see the long entry where my mom had lovingly placed various family photos of us throughout the years. Camilla's pigtails in kindergarten and her toothless grin in first grade. A picture of the four of us in San Francisco, the Golden Gate Bridge behind us. The two of us in our prom dresses and graduation caps and gowns.

So many memories and not a single one was devoid of my beloved sister.

"It's a little hard," I whispered to Levi, but my gaze remained locked on the house. "There's so much past inside there, so many memories of Camilla, and God, Levi, it just makes me miss her so much."

He grasped my fingers tighter and lifted them to his mouth for a soft kiss.

I swallowed hard against the thick emotion clogging my throat and blinked away the tears that threatened to spill from my lids.

I didn't want to be a mess in front of my parents. I wanted to be strong for them.

I wasn't the only one who had lost someone important.

They'd lost their daughter. Their child. Their baby girl.

I could only imagine the grief and sadness they'd had to process over the past month and a half. Especially since I hadn't done my part in giving them glimpses of the daughter they still had left.

"It's okay to be sad, Ivy," he said, his voice soft and soothing. "It's okay to cry and grieve. I know you're probably sitting here trying to be strong, but you know what I think you should do?"

"What?" I asked and turned my head to meet his warm eyes.

"I think you should just let yourself feel whatever your feeling," he responded, reaching out with his free hand to brush a loose strand of hair behind my ear. "This is your home and those are your parents and, if anything, you being completely real with them will only give all three of you the freedom to process and grieve and just be."

Such wise words from a man who used to live his life with avoidance in mind.

I marveled at how far Levi had come since I'd first met him.

I'd thought about how he'd lived with all those secrets and sadness and endless guilt buried deep within his soul and how it had been those very things that were keeping him from really living.

He had gone through so much, seen so much, dealt with so much, and yet, here he was, being my biggest and strongest confidant.

I couldn't have survived the tragic loss of my sister without him. I knew that much.

He had been the one constant that helped hold me together, that helped pick up the broken pieces when I really lost it.

"Okay," I whispered and let go of his hand. "Let's go inside."

With a big inhale and a deep exhale, I cleansed myself of my worries and fears and got out of the car with one thing in mind—*just be in the moment.*

It only took two soft knocks at the door for my mother's smiling face to meet my eyes.

"Ivy," she said, and her voice sounded relieved and happy and sad all at once. "Oh my gosh, I've missed you." She stepped out onto the porch and wrapped me up in her arms, and I never even considered stopping the tears produced by the comfort of her embrace.

My tears unchecked and unashamed, I let the salty liquid stream down my cheeks and onto her shirt as I buried my face into her neck and hugged her as tightly as I could. "I've missed you too, Mom. It's been so hard. So, so hard."

She leaned back and placed both of her hands on my cheeks. "I know, sweetie. Your dad and I have been a mess too."

"Dad?" I questioned through a sob. Dave Stone was the strongest guy I knew and the steel in my spine. He was everything I wanted to be and more, and the thought of him bowing under the pressure of the grief made my head spin.

Still, for some reason, it made me feel better. If someone that strong was struggling, I had all the reason in the world to be struggling too.

My mom nodded, a sad smile curving the line of her peachy,

coral-colored lips. "Some days, it feels impossible to get out of bed knowing I have to live inside a world without Camilla, but I know in my heart she would want us to find peace. She would want us to grieve, but she'd also want us to find the strength to move past our sadness."

I nodded, and more tears slipped from my lids. "I know...it's just...I miss her so much."

She swiped the liquid emotion off my skin with her thumbs. "Of course you do, sweetie. She was your identical twin. You two shared a bond like no other."

"I love you, Mom." I hugged her tight. "I love you so much."

She leaned back to look at me, tears stinging in her eyes now. "I love you too, sweetheart," she whispered. "I think we'll get through this. It's the hardest thing I've ever done, and God, I miss her so much, but I think we'll get through it."

"I think so too."

It was the first time I really, truly felt like that was a possibility.

"Where's Dad?" I asked, and she glanced over her shoulder as we released each other from our embrace.

"He's out on the deck cooking up some steaks for us. Please tell me you guys are hungry because he hasn't stopped cooking all day." She smiled at me and then moved her eyes to Levi. "And, Levi, honey, it is so good to see you," she said and stepped forward to give him a quick, tight hug. "I'm so happy you've been staying in LA with my Ivy. I know she really needs you right now." A rolling gurgle caught in her throat as she bottled a small cry and said words I knew I wasn't meant to hear. "Thank you so much for bringing her back to us."

I dabbed at the corner of my eye to stave off the guilty tingle, and I looked to Levi. His soft eyes and warm smile were on me, and they were annoyingly self-vindicating.

"*We* wouldn't want to be anywhere else."

The know-it-all bastard.

"Let's go out back. Maybe you can talk some sense into your father. He seems to think we've got thirty people coming and needs to prepare a buffet worthy of a king."

I smiled, and God, it felt good to just smile. Somehow, seeing my mom doing the same made it feel normal.

Levi wrapped his arm around my shoulders, and we followed my mom inside and straight back through the main center hall of the house.

The instant we stepped out onto the deck, I spotted my dad, standing in front of the grill and tapping his toes to the sounds of Bob Seger's "Night Moves" playing from his phone.

"Dave, we've got company," my mom informed him. Chagrined by information he so very obviously knew—as he'd spent all day grilling to be ready for us—my dad glanced over his shoulder, smiled fleetingly at my mom, and then rolled his eyes to me.

Still, the sight of me must have been a healing balm for sore eyes because knowing we were coming didn't diminish his excitement at all.

"Ivy Lou!" he exclaimed and quickly set his metal spatula on the side of the grill. "God, girl, it's good to see you," he said as he walked toward me.

It took mere seconds before I was wrapped up into one of his big bear hugs.

"Hi, Dad," I said, and he leaned back to meet my eyes. "Missed you."

"Missed you too, baby girl," he murmured softly, giving me a teasing gleam of his eye. "Even in this blond, unrecognizable form of the daughter I thought I knew." He hugged me tightly again and then moved his gaze to Levi.

"Officer Fox," he said with a teasing grin. "I hope you're not here to inspect my deck and grill to see if they're up to our HOA code. Because I can assure you, they are definitely not. Also, it was all

Helen's idea."

My mom laughed, and Levi grinned.

"I'm off duty, sir," he said. "Honestly, I might be off duty permanently."

My dad quirked a brow, and Levi responded by wrapping his arm around my shoulders, tucking me close to his side, and smiling down at me.

"I need to stay close to my girl."

A little *aww* left my mom's lips, and my dad smiled like the damn sun.

"That's good to hear, son," my father said. "That's real good to hear. I'm glad the two of you have found happiness between all of the pain you've had to face. Both of you deserve it. You deserve to be happy."

My dad's words hit me straight in the chest.

I hadn't felt like I'd deserved to be happy. I couldn't even find a passable avenue to the *idea* of it.

Losing my sister had been the worst and hardest thing I'd ever been through.

But maybe someday, I'd be able to replace the pain with peace, and I wouldn't feel any guilt or shame in that. My parents seemed to be doing the best they could, and I had to give myself the same grace.

"Did you guys have any trouble on your way in?" my mom asked, and I raised a confused brow.

"Trouble?"

"With the paparazzi trying to follow you here."

"No." I shook my head and sighed at the same time. "We did the whole shell game thing and did a quick vehicle switch inside of an empty warehouse after we left the hotel."

The paparazzi issue was becoming a really hard obstacle for us.

Wherever we went, they followed. And they were ruthless when it came to getting photos of us. Climbing fences, standing on top of parked cars, running into the middle of traffic, there wasn't anything they wouldn't do.

It was scary.

And because of that fact, Levi had amped up our security from just Baylor and Hampton to another two-man team when we went anywhere.

I was used to photogs and people wanting to get my picture, but since everything had happened with Camilla and the movie, Levi and I had become a huge target for the media.

They wanted to know and see and witness anything and everything they could.

"Has the press backed off on you and Dad?" I asked, and Mom shrugged.

"It's gotten a little better. Not nonexistent, of course, but better."

I sighed. I hated that while my parents were trying to grieve, they had journalists attempting to contact them and ask them a million questions about our lives.

The mere idea of it made me feel itchy and a bit stabby if I was being honest.

The only thing that kept me sane was the fact that they lived inside of a gated community and didn't have those fucking vultures standing on their lawn.

"I know your mother is quite the beauty, but I'm sure our fifteen minutes of fame will be up soon, Ivy. So, don't even start worrying your pretty little head about it," my dad said and then added, "It's just too bad the sudden fame isn't revolving around something else, like my grilling skills. In my opinion, those are worthy of a front-page spread. I mean, look at those steaks." He pointed toward the grill.

"A true masterpiece, sir," Levi said, amusement in his voice, and I smiled.

FOX

"Like the Picasso of meat, Dad. They almost look too good to eat."

"Don't put ideas in his head, Ivy!" my mom exclaimed. "Next thing I know, I'll have a museum of Plexiglass-covered steaks in the basement."

"Now that would give the press something to talk about, hun," my dad said with a wink, and my mom couldn't not laugh.

While my parents teased one another and my dad took the steaks off the grill, I looked up at Levi and smiled. "I'm glad we came."

"Me too," he said.

"And thank you."

"For what?" he asked, and his eyes searched mine.

I pressed a kiss to his lips. "For being you. And for forcing me to do what I needed all along."

CHAPTER
ELEVEN

Levi

May 15th, 2016

L AST NIGHT, I'D WATCHED IVY THRIVE WITHIN HER PARENTS' comfortable and loving web of company. I'd watched her cry and grieve too, but mostly, I'd seen her smile and laugh and just be the feisty, quick-witted, beautiful woman I loved so much.

I couldn't remember the last time I'd seen Ivy really laugh or smile like she had while joking around with her dad.

The evening had been so needed, we hadn't gotten back to the hotel until well after midnight. And the instant Ivy's head had hit the pillow, she'd been out like a light. The complete opposite of the restless nights that had become a constant for her since Camilla's death.

God, it had been a rough month and a half.

So much tragedy.

So many obstacles.

So much pain.

I'd seen Ivy at her lowest of lows. I'd seen her break down. I'd seen her lose control. I'd seen her unable to control her emotions and impulsively lash out.

But after last night, to me, it felt like something was slowly changing inside of her.

FOX

And it gave me hope.

I stared out the window of the bedroom. The white curtains were pulled off to the side, and the sun's first rays cresting the horizon hinted at its arrival.

I glanced over at the alarm clock on the nightstand and saw it was only a little after seven in the morning.

Considering I hadn't actually fallen asleep until a little after two, it was probably way too early to be awake. But I was a creature of habit. I blamed years of early morning patrol shifts.

Ivy, on the other hand, wasn't much of an early riser and would probably sleep until noon if I let her.

She stirred beside me in the bed, and I turned on my side to look at her.

Her long lashes fanned down over her cheeks, and her lips were slightly parted as soft, steady breaths moved in and out of her lungs.

As I drank her in, my gaze staring in complete awe of her beauty, I was certain I'd never grow tired of this. I'd love this woman for the rest of my life. I was sure of it. She was the one and only person I wanted to love for the rest of my days and nights.

Hell, I wasn't sure a lifetime with Ivy would be enough, but I sure as fuck would try to make the best of it. And, one day in the hopefully near future, I was going to marry this woman.

I was going to put my ring on her finger, and a few years down the road, I was going to put my babies in her belly.

My heart was hers.

Ivy belonged with me.

And, no doubt, I belonged with her.

I brushed a soft strand of blond hair from her forehead, and even though her eyelashes fluttered a little in response, her body stayed lax in sleep.

God, I would do anything for this woman.

I'd permanently quit the police force.

I'd move to California.

I'd start from scratch if it meant being with her for forever.

And the craziest thing of all, those things—that used to be big things—only paled in comparison to what it meant to have Ivy in my life.

I wanted and needed and loved her with everything I had.

Leaning forward, I pressed a soft kiss to her mouth because I couldn't help myself.

When I pulled back, I found Ivy's sleepy green eyes staring back at me.

"What are you doing?" she asked, voice raspy with sleep.

"Kissing you."

"Isn't it a little early for kisses, Levi?"

I shook my head. "There's never a bad time when it comes to kissing you."

Ivy giggled at that and glanced over my shoulder to check the time. "Jesus, it's like seven in the morning. It's way too early to be awake right now."

"Speak for yourself, night owl," I retorted. "This feels like sleeping in to me."

She groaned and turned over on her other side, her back facing me. "Let me sleep, you crazy person."

I moved toward her and wrapped my arm around her front, pulling her warm little body back against my chest. "I think you should wake up," I whispered into her ear.

A few moments of silence filled the room, and I just cuddled her body into mine and savored the feel of her within my embrace.

I was fully prepared for her to moan and groan and try to swat me away, but to my surprise, Ivy turned back around, and those pretty green eyes of hers locked with mine.

"Hi," she whispered, and I smiled.

Blond hair a mess, eyes still a little sleepy, and face natural, she was so fucking beautiful it damn near made my chest ache.

"Hi, baby."

"I actually slept last night," she said, and I nodded.

"You did. I'm glad. I know you needed it."

"I even dreamed."

I quirked a brow. "Oh, really? What'd you dream about?"

She was quiet for a long moment and she worried her lip with her teeth, but eventually, she opened up to me. "I had a dream about Camilla. We were sitting inside the kitchen of our house. Here in LA, I mean. I was cooking breakfast for us, eggs and bacon and coffee. And she just looked and sounded so damn happy. I don't even remember what we were talking about in the dream, but it felt so real, Levi. It felt so, so real. Do you think that's possible?" she asked. "Do you think our loved ones can come talk to us through our dreams?"

"Yeah, actually, I do," I answered honestly. After Grace had died, I'd had more than a few dreams like that.

"Me too," she whispered and rubbed her little nose against mine. "Can we do something today?"

"What did you have in mind?"

"I know it's going to take some arranging with security and transportation and I know I'm going to have to wear some sort of disguise because of the stupid paparazzi, but today, I want to get out and enjoy the sun. And mostly, I want to take some flowers to Camilla's grave."

"I like this plan," I said because I did.

Ivy hadn't been to her sister's gravesite since the funeral. It hadn't been out of neglect. She just wasn't ready.

But today, she was, and I felt so much relief in that. Like we were really rounding a corner toward her new normal.

And, as odd as it might have sounded to someone else, I felt like the luckiest son of a bitch on the planet because I'd get to be there for Ivy, at the cemetery.

Often regarded as creepy or uncomfortable, they weren't the natural order of a place of worship. Thanks to my history with Grace, their expansive space felt different to me.

It was sacred and loving, and it was as close to holy as I'd ever get.

And today's visit—the first visit—would mean even more.

I would get to watch her pick out flowers for her sister. I would be the one to soothe her anxious chatter in the car on our way there. The one who would get to hold her nervous hand as we walked toward Camilla's grave.

I was her man. Her shoulder to cry on. Her pillar of strength in her times of weakness. And her biggest fucking cheerleader.

I was certain no man had ever loved a woman as much as I loved Ivy, and together, today, we'd share a moment with Camilla—and God.

CHAPTER
TWELVE

Ivy

ROWS OF TOMBSTONES STOOD ERECT IN STILLNESS TO THE LEFT and right, in front and behind, like a silent city of tribute for loved ones who had left this life. Some were crumbled from weathering and age, while others were smooth marble with pristine words engraved into the stone and laid with beautiful floral tributes, no doubt placed thoughtfully by loved ones.

The cemetery was neat and tidy and clean. Manicured grass and perfectly landscaped garden beds with small benches for mourners to sit and process their emotions.

Thick ivy and rose bushes were an obvious staple throughout, and Camilla would have hated the gardeners' preference in flowers. She pretty much despised roses, especially pink ones. She always said they were too clichéd. When she'd helped me choose flowers for our house last year, she'd all but demanded I have the landscapers plant wild flowers and Japanese cherry blossoms and a whole bunch of other flowers that were eclectic and unique and even a bit obscure.

I nearly laughed at just how much she would have bitched about those fucking pink roses as I walked toward her grave.

Levi walked beside me, his fingers intertwined with mine.

Silence stretched between us, but it was a peaceful silence. A thoughtful quietness meant to let me process and feel.

The instant I spotted the smooth marble of her gravestone, scattered thoughts and bittersweet memories of Camilla morphed into acute sadness.

By the time I reached her grave, a bouquet of wild daisies and sunflowers gripped tightly in my hands, tears flowed unchecked down my cheeks. Wild and numerous, they dripped off my chin and onto my shirt, soaking the fabric enough to stick it to my skin.

I was too sad to actually cry or sob, so I just stood there, still as a statue, holding tightly to Levi's hand while the magnitude of Camilla's loss swept over me.

The word sad sounded so childish, like something flimsy, something someone should be able to cast off with a happy thought or smile or hug. But *this* kind of sad, a raw, aching melancholy, was nothing of the sort. It sat inside my veins like a germ seed of depression, just waiting for the right conditions to grow, to send out roots that threatened to choke the hope out of my heart.

And, God, did my heart ache.

It throbbed. It stung. It twisted and turned erratically. Whenever Camilla's death really hit me, it felt like someone had reached inside my chest with a meat hook and shredded my heart to near pieces.

Right now, the realization of her loss hit me hard.

I let go of Levi's hand slowly, the tingle of the newly released nerves alerting me to just how tight a grip I'd had on it, and sat down in front of her grave.

Levi gave me the space and the silence I needed to get my thoughts together.

Fingers skimming, I touched the curves of her name in the stone and swallowed.

"God, I miss you, Cami," I whispered, the smooth silk of my voice cracked by the constant flow of tears. "I miss you so much that some days I can hardly get myself out of bed. Some days..." I shook my head and pressed my palm flat to the cool stone. "Some days it feels *impossible* to live in a world without you in it."

I set the bouquet beside her gravestone and stared down at the freshly cut grass. I ran my fingers through the manicured blades and silently wondered if my sister could hear me or see me or feel me.

Just then, the warmest, softest breeze blew past me and urged goose bumps onto my skin.

I hope it's a sign.

"I dreamed about you last night," I went on, hoping if I kept talking to her, she'd give me something else to know she was there. "I can't tell you how good it felt to see your smiling face again. To talk to you and laugh with you and make you eggs. I hope you'll keep coming to see me in my dreams. It makes me feel so close to you. It makes me feel like you're still here."

I reached out and ran my fingers across the letters of her engraved name again.

"Levi and I had dinner with Mom and Dad last night," I whispered. "They miss you too, Cami. So much. So, so much. We spent most of the night reminiscing about our happiest memories with you." I laughed. "There were some good ones. Like the time you snuck out to meet Tommy Tiller for an overnight date and then came home with his blood on your knuckles because he tried to get up your skirt. Dad still thinks it's one of his proudest moments as a father."

A shaky sigh escaped my lips, and my tears slowed until they no longer flowed down my cheeks in waves, instead, only shining my eyes and fogging my vision a little.

I blinked past the emotion and lifted my arm up to swipe the residual dampness from my cheeks.

"You'll always be a part of me, Cam. Even though you're not physically here, you're still in my heart. You're my sister. My identical twin. My soul's other half. No matter how much time passes, those things will never change."

I stood up from my spot in the grass and rested my fingertips on top of her gravestone. "I'm sorry this happened to you and I'm sorry I couldn't protect you and I'm sorry it was my career that brought this tragedy into our lives. It's been really hard for me to wrap my brain around the fact that you aren't alive because you were my identical twin. And it's been even harder to comprehend that my sister, my best friend, my favorite person in the whole wide world willingly sacrificed her life for mine. I am so thankful and so fucking *mad* that you did that. But I know, if the roles had been reversed, I would have done the same thing for you."

Just saying those words out loud urged what felt like a thousand pounds to lift from my shoulders. Instantly, I knew coming to visit my sister's grave was the best, most rational decision I'd made in weeks.

If anything, it made me feel closer to her. It helped me search for the much-needed peace and closure. I had a feeling it would be a very long time before I'd ever really find peace in anything related to losing my sister, but it was important that I searched for it.

"I hope you'll keep visiting me in my dreams. I love you so much, sis. And I miss you even more."

After one long, quiet gaze down at her gravestone, I turned on my heels and searched the space adjacent. Levi sat several feet behind me, on a bench beneath a big oak tree.

His eyes never left mine as I closed the distance. "You okay?" he asked when I stopped in front of him. I nodded.

"I'm getting there, but I'm really happy I came here today."

"I'm glad to hear that, baby." He offered a soft, wistful smile and got to his feet.

One of his strong arms wrapped around my shoulders, he led us back toward the waiting SUV, and the instant we got inside, he gripped my hand in his.

"Should we grab some breakfast?" he asked, but before I could answer, my phone started ringing loudly from inside the purse at my feet.

I pulled my cell out of the front pocket and checked the screen.

Incoming Call: Mariah

A quick accept and I pressed the phone to my ear. "Hey, Mariah. How are you?"

"Listen, I have good news," she said, bypassing greetings altogether.

Good news? That seemed like a fucking oxymoron these days.

"What are you talking about?"

"I got you a meeting with someone who is very willing to talk to you about your quest to stop *Cold* from being released to the public," she said.

"Really?" I asked, and my brow rose up to my forehead in surprised excitement. "Who?"

"June Gatto." The name immediately clicked into place in my mind.

June Gatto. The screenwriter on *Cold*.

Holy shit. That *was* good news.

"Seriously?"

"Can you be at her office Friday at two?"

"Yes."

"Well, then it looks like you've got a pair of willing ears that will hopefully understand your concerns about *Cold* being released to the world."

Thank God.

We ended our call shortly after that, and Levi looked over at me, his brow raised in curiosity. "What's going on?"

"June Gatto, the screenwriter on *Cold*. We've got a meeting with her Friday," I said, and it only confused him more.

"Is Mariah going with you?"

I shook my head. "No, but I'm hoping you will. I really need you there, Levi."

I'd made the mistake of trying to go it alone before, but I was done with that now. I needed his support and guidance.

"You want me to go to the meeting with you?"

"Not want, Levi. *Need*. I need you there."

He leaned forward and kissed my forehead softly. "Then, I wouldn't miss it for anything."

Celebrity EXTRA
Ivy Stone Spotted at Her Sister's Gravesite

May 16th, 2016

The sun was shining down on a newly blond Ivy Stone as she sat beside her sister's gravesite after placing a beautiful bouquet of wild flowers and sunflowers in tribute yesterday.

An inside source revealed she stayed at the cemetery for an hour or so, before leaving hand in hand with her boyfriend, Levi Fox.

Later in the day, paparazzi spotted them enjoying a breakfast on La Sur's terrace. Ivy appeared happy and at ease while she ate her meal and chatted with her boyfriend over pancakes and coffee.

This leaves us all wondering and hoping that the Ivy Stone we've come to know and love is slowly finding herself again amid the tragic loss of her sister, Camilla.

CHAPTER
THIRTEEN

Levi

May 20th, 2016

I'D ONLY BEEN IN LA FOR A COUPLE OF MONTHS, BUT I'D QUICKLY found out the traffic here was a fucking mess. We'd left the hotel over an hour ago, and what should have been a quick, twenty-minute drive had turned into sitting in gridlocked traffic for nearly forty-five minutes.

The driver headed down the ramp to the parking garage located in downtown LA, and Ivy fidgeted beside me. Her knee bounced erratically, and she kept tapping the tips of her fingers across the top of her black dress pants.

She was a little ball of nervous tension and anxiety.

The anticipation of meeting with *Cold's* screenwriter in hopes that someone could assist with her desire to stop the movie from being released to the public had gifted Ivy with another night of restless sleep.

Her exhaustion showed through the soft, dark circles under her eyes and the raspy, tired tone of her voice.

But it was apparent she wasn't thinking about being tired or wanting to go back to bed right now. She was far too amped up, and adrenaline had taken over.

FOX

The SUV pulled to a stop in front of the basement entrance of the garage, and I looked over at Ivy. She worried her teeth against her lip ruthlessly, cutting at the delicate skin with the sharp point of her canine. I reached out to steady her still-tapping fingers and hopefully curtail the damage to her lip.

"You ready?"

A deep sigh escaped her lungs. "I guess I'm as ready as I'll ever be."

I clasped her hand in mine. "Just remember that no matter what happens, no matter what the outcome is, we're going to get through it, okay?"

She nodded, resolute. "Okay."

A minute later, we were out of the vehicle and in the elevator.

And a few minutes after that, June Gatto's assistant greeted us at the entrance of the sixth floor.

"Hi, I'm Fiona," she said, standing in the entryway, her body clad in a pristine business suit and her hair pulled up in a tight bun. Her voice, her smile—it was all fake and phony, but I'd become accustomed to that kind of bullshit since I'd been staying in LA with Ivy.

I was a man who'd take blunt over sugarcoated any fucking day of the week, and the insincere smiles and pretentious behavior grated on my goddamn nerves.

"June is in her office finishing up a last-minute conference call, but she'll be ready shortly," she updated as she led us into an open and airy room where lush couches, clear glass tables, and big potted plants highlighted the space. "Please, sit down, make yourselves comfortable." She gestured toward the room. "Can I get you anything to drink while you wait? Espresso? A glass of champagne?"

A glass of fucking champagne?

Jesus Christ, these people lived in a fantasy world.

Both Ivy and I declined and sat down on one of the cream velvet sofas.

I looked around the space and tried to picture a man like Chief Pulse in a room like this. He would've damn near had a stroke hearing someone offer champagne at a business meeting, much less fucking espresso.

I nearly laughed at the thought.

Ivy picked up a magazine from the table, but she quickly threw it back onto the glass surface with a sigh.

I glanced down to find the magazine in question—a fucking gossip rag—actually had her face splashed across it. The headline read: *Ivy Stone's Secret Battle with Depression.*

Secret battle with depression? What a load of fucking bullshit.

This woman was grieving the death of her sister. A death that had occurred at the hands of a man who had a sick fascination with Ivy. If that didn't push anyone toward some emotional trauma, I didn't know what would.

Yet this celebrity gossip magazine felt it was their right to use someone's pain to increase their fucking readership.

It was completely messed up.

Anger filtered into my veins and tingled inside my hands. I flexed my fingers against the discomfort and did my best to push the emotion away.

Now wasn't the time to let anger and rage fester, especially over a goddamn gossip magazine I had no control over.

I was here to be a pillar of support for Ivy, not get her worked up even more than she already was.

With a strong and steady hand, I reached out and patted the top of Ivy's bouncing knee. She glanced over at me, and a pitiful laugh left her lungs.

"I swear, I'll be less insane once this meeting is over," she said in spite of herself. "It's making me so anxious. I just don't want it to end up the same way as the meeting with the studio head."

I smiled at that. "Baby, you don't have to explain anything to me.

Be as insane as you want."

A real smile crested her lips. "Now, I think you might be asking for trouble right there."

I chuckled softly. "I'll take as much of your trouble as I can get."

Her green eyes searched mine, and eventually, she whispered, "Thank you for being here."

I wrapped my arm around her shoulders and pressed a soft kiss to her hair. "I will always be here for you. Never forget that."

A soft sigh escaped her lungs, and she rested her head against my shoulder, and the quiet, peaceful silence spread into an otherwise emotionally chaotic moment.

But it ended as quickly as it started.

Fiona stepped into the room, smiling like the three of us were fucking family.

It was a sham of a smile and made my stomach churn with discomfort.

"June is ready for you," she said and gestured toward the opposite side of the room where a short hallway opened. "If you'll follow me, I'll take you to her office."

We walked behind her, down the marble-floored hallway until we reached what I assumed was the screenwriter's office.

Fiona opened the door, and both Ivy and I stepped inside.

"June," she announced. "I have Ivy Stone here for you."

The woman turned around in her chair, and the instant my gaze met the features of her face, I felt like I was having an out-of-body experience.

My stomach fell like a rock, straight through my body and into my shoes, and a sharp, painful intake of breath filled my lungs.

Ivy, unaware of the shrapnel spinning wildly from my mind, continued walking into the room toward the leather chairs on the opposite end of the big glass desk.

I...I couldn't move my legs.

I was paralyzed and poisoned as years of life fled from my body and heart and slammed me right back into the mind of a boy.

A boy who hadn't been ready to be a man.

Glancing back to pull me closer as she sat, Ivy finally noticed my distance. Her brow furrowed down, eyes searching mine erratically.

The woman behind the desk hadn't stopped looking at me. Not for one moment, not for one second. Ivy wasn't even here as far as she was concerned.

Big blue eyes. Jet-black hair. The same nose. All of the familiar qualities were nearly too real to process, but I could tell she'd weathered the time well.

She looked uncertain and unsure, but eventually, she quelled the silence. "Levi," the stranger said my name like it was a prayer, and it only took hearing that one word from her lips to confirm everything.

June Gatto wasn't just the screenwriter on *Cold*.

June Gatto was June *Fox*.

My fucking mom.

The woman who'd abandoned our family when I was just a child.

The woman I hadn't seen or heard from in years.

The woman I used to cry myself to sleep over when I was a kid, hoping and praying she'd come back to us.

The fucking awful woman who'd torn my family apart and changed my father irreparably. He'd never been a kind, caring man, but he'd been tolerable. After she'd left, I'd lost everything.

"Do you—Do you two know each other?" Ivy asked, glancing back and forth between us in confusion.

"She's my mother," I said without pretense. I'd have loved to make it more complicated or eased into the blow, but the words were spoken for me from a place I didn't recognize. A place where the world kept hitting, blow after blow, until you couldn't hold up your head anymore.

"W-what?" Ivy's eyes grew wide as saucers at my words. "This is your mom?"

My shock quickly morphed into rage, and I stepped forward until I stood directly in front of her desk.

"You're fucking June Gatto?" I questioned, my voice rising with each word. "You're the screenwriter for *Cold?*"

"I'm sorry you had to find out this way," she responded, and I felt Ivy's presence move beside me. "I didn't know you were coming to this meeting. Otherwise, I would have handled it differently."

"Handled it differently?" I questioned, and my jaw ticked with rage. "What the fuck does that even mean?"

"I wouldn't have let it happen like this."

"You mean you wouldn't have let it happen at all," I retorted, sarcasm dripping from my voice like a faucet. A sharp gasp left her mouth at my words, but I didn't stop. I didn't hold back. I had twenty plus years of pain and trauma from this woman, and I sure as fuck wasn't going to stand there and make this easy on her when she hadn't given a fuck about making anything easy on me.

Me.

Her son.

Her only child. Well, at least, I thought I was her only child. For all I knew, she'd replaced us with a shiny new family that met her selfish fucking needs. "I mean, we both know your track record, *Mom.* When it comes to me, you're the master of the disappearing act."

"I'm sorry I left, Levi, but I had to. I couldn't survive in that small town. I couldn't stay there with your father. He...he didn't leave room for anyone else."

"Oh, but it was perfectly fine for you to leave your kid to suffer through it?" I tossed back. "You do realize what my father was like after you left, right? You realize that he didn't magically turn into a loving guy? Disconnected, narcissistic. If it weren't for Sam Murphy and Red Pulse, I'd have had to fend for myself. All because of you."

The sham of a woman that was my mother stood up from her seat, and her eyes stared back at me earnestly. She looked sad and pained, and I didn't care to see any of it. I refused to feel any sort of sympathy for her discomfort.

"I had no idea," she whispered. "I had no idea it was like that for you. If I would've known—"

"You mean if you would've cared to know," I cut her off before she could give me some line of bullshit about how she would have done things differently. "Christ, how could you think it would be anything else?" I shook my head. "You just didn't give a shit about anyone else but yourself."

"I do care, Levi. I still care."

The realization of all that this meant slapped me across the face, and my head swam with the fact that she was the fucking screenwriter. The person who had made my real-life hell into a goddamn movie.

"All this fucking time. All this time and you're the one who did this to me? You're the one who sensationalized one of the worst moments of my life into a goddamn movie for other people's entertainment? Do you even understand how completely fucked that is? How fucking cruel that is?"

She shook her head. "That's not why I did it, Levi. I did it for you—to help you, not to hurt you."

A shocked laugh left my lips. "To help me? Oh, that's rich. Please, explain to me how you thought this movie would help me."

"You needed to face it, Levi," she said. "Red sent me updates…" She stuttered as my face turned stormy, and then she lowered her voice cautiously. "…for a while. He stopped. Honestly, I think he was hoping I would come back." Her throat quivered. "I couldn't face you. Even then, I knew you wouldn't take my appearance well. I *knew* you wouldn't want to see me. I knew my presence would just hurt you," she said, and my skin crawled at the sight of actual tears in her eyes. Did she think a few measly pools of liquid regret could really erase what my life had been like as a result of her selfishness?

"And why the hell might that be, Mom? Why wouldn't I want to see the woman who left me for her own gain?" I snapped.

She twisted her lips. "I guess…I guess it was why I wrote the screenplay for this story. Sure, it's about Grace. But for me, it was always about you. It was so hard seeing the tragedy that you had to live through on the news and in the papers. And I just…I just—"

"Two fucking times," I cut her off. I didn't need or want to hear another word of her bullshit excuses or reasons. "This is twice you've *ruined* my fucking life," I said, vibrating with the power of my words.

I felt Ivy's presence beside me shift closer, a soft hand settling on my shoulder.

That gentle hand of hers was the only thing keeping me steady.

"Do you even understand what this movie has done? The pain and trauma and tragedy that've occurred because of it?" I questioned, and my voice started to rise again.

I thought about Dane and Camilla.

I remembered the way Boyce had looked when I'd walked into the house and he'd had a knife to Camilla's throat.

But, unbidden as it was, I also thought about how if it hadn't been for that fucking movie, I never would have met Ivy.

It was irony and pain and bittersweet all rolled up into one giant confusing clusterfuck of emotions.

I didn't really know what to say or do after that.

I just stood there, frozen to my spot, staring at a woman I *should've* known, but was a complete stranger in my eyes.

Ivy's hand squeezed my shoulder, and I glanced down to find her looking up at me, her big green eyes filled with so much concern it made my chest ache.

She'd come here for a reason.

And it sure as fuck wasn't so I could be painfully reunited with my absent mother.

"Stop the movie," I blurted out and met my mom's eyes. "If you really want to help me. If you really want to do something for me, your fucking son, then don't let this film be released."

"I-I wish I could, Levi," she said, and her voice was soft with sadness. "I really wish I could. But I can't. I've tried. But the contracts that were signed give the studio full control over what happens with this movie. I've already had my lawyers scour through every detail, and there is nothing anyone can do."

"Wow," I muttered and shook my head. "Well, I hope it was all worth it, Mom. I hope you're enjoying your Hollywood life. I hope you've gotten everything you wished for. Money. Success. Zero parental responsibilities. Or shit, maybe you have other kids. Whatever this brand-new life of yours entails, I hope it's everything you ever dreamed of."

Her mouth turned down at the corners. "Levi—"

"No." I lifted my hand. "I don't want to hear anything you're about to say. Your words mean shit to me. And you sure as fuck don't deserve any more of my or Ivy's time."

"Levi...I'm so sorry," she said. "I'm so sorry."

This time, I completely ignored her. From now on, I only had eyes for Ivy.

"I need to leave," I said.

"I know," she whispered back and grasped my hand in hers.

"Levi...wait..." June Gatto moved around her big fucking desk and tried to stop us, but I was done.

Done with talking.

Done with feeling.

Done with her.

CHAPTER
FOURTEEN

Ivy

MY HEAD SWAM, AND MY CHEST WAS SO TIGHT I COULD BARELY breathe against the crushing anxiety. I felt like I was in some sort of alternate universe where I wasn't even in my body. Like I was just a mere spectator of my actual self, standing off to the side watching my own life like a movie.

A movie that was more car crash and tragedy than anything else.

I barely remembered leaving June Gatto's office.

The drive back to the hotel had felt both long and fast, the realization of time too hard to comprehend over the shock of what I'd just witnessed.

And I really had no idea how long we'd been back inside our hotel room.

It could have been minutes. Hell, it could have been hours for all I knew.

The world spun erratically around me, and I gripped the couch cushion with my fingertips in a pathetic attempt to steady myself.

Levi paced around the room like a caged animal desperate to be released from his confined hell.

His eyes were empty, his lips stuck in a perpetual firm line, and his jaw was so hard I feared it might shatter if it grew any tenser.

He strode over toward the small dining table and abruptly swiped his hands across it, knocking everything off the surface and onto the floor.

"Fuck!" he shouted. I grimaced when the booming vibration of his yell rolled through my ears.

He had so many emotions undulating throughout his body, he didn't know what to do with himself.

I couldn't blame him.

He deserved to be angry. He deserved to throw shit and scream and shout.

He deserved to feel whatever it was he was feeling.

Considering, as of late, I'd had more than my fair share of break-downs, I completely understood, and I felt nothing but sadness that he had to go through this.

The realization that June Gatto was in fact June Fox was almost too much to wrap my mind around.

His mother, the woman who had left him when he was a child, had written a movie that revealed his innermost pain.

Because she'd written that screenplay, he'd had to relive every-thing that had happened with Grace. I couldn't understand how any-one would have thought that was anything but cruel. How a mother could've thought that was the right thing to do for her son.

A strangled sob left his lungs, and he sat down on one of the dining chairs and put his head in his hands. His body vibrated and his shoulders shook, and my heart felt like it was breaking into a million tiny pieces at the agonized sight of him.

How much tragedy and pain did one person deserve in a lifetime?

I felt like Levi had reached his quota over six years ago, but ap-parently, life was hell-bent on making him experience the maximum amount one human being could possibly handle.

And, God, I hated seeing him like this. Normally so strong, so fucking strong, and right now, I had never seen him more vulnerable.

Tears pricked behind my eyes, and I stood up from the couch and moved toward him.

I couldn't let him deal with this alone.

I needed to be there for him.

I *wanted* to be there for him.

He'd been so good to me over the past few months. He'd let me grieve and feel and just mourn Camilla's death without any judgment. He'd let me lash out and pick fights and lose my fucking mind, and all he'd given back in return was patience and love.

I'd needed him so badly, and he'd never hesitated to drop everything to be there.

He'd left Montana for me.

He'd taken a leave of absence from the police force for me.

And he'd never once made me feel like I was a burden.

No, if anything, he made me feel like he hadn't wanted to be anywhere else. Even during the hard times, the sad times, the fucking terrible, insane times where I was quite seriously losing my shit.

Levi had done all of that *for* me.

And now, he deserved the same *from* me.

I placed my hand on his shoulder, and he looked up at me, emotion dampening his cheeks and reddening his eyes.

"I'm sorry, Ivy," he whispered. "It's just too much to process right now. All of it. I just…I just can't…" He paused, and I shook my head.

"You don't have to explain anything to me," I whispered back. "God, Levi, I'm so sorry you had to deal with that today. Deal with *her.*"

His mother's name felt like it weighed one hundred pounds, and I didn't even have the strength to push it past my lips.

"I'm sorry you had to see it. You already have enough fucking bullshit on your plate without adding my baggage into the mix."

"Pretty sure my baggage has been your baggage for the past couple of months. So…" I said softly and offered an apologetic smile.

His blue eyes lifted ever so slightly at the corners, and I urged his arms open so I could sit down on his lap, my thighs straddling his.

I pressed both of my hands to his cheeks and swiped away a few rogue tears with my thumbs. "I'm sorry you had such a shitty mother. You deserved better than that."

"I did, didn't I?"

I nodded. "You still do."

"I never want to see her again, Ivy," he whispered. "If I don't have to see or speak to that woman for the rest of my life, it would still be too soon. She isn't my mom. She is a complete stranger, just some woman I happen to share the same genes with."

"You don't have to see her again," I said softly. "It's your choice to keep toxic people out of your life. I know I sure as hell won't be accepting any acting jobs when her name is written across the screenplay, and I'll make sure everyone on my team knows not to give out any of your information if she happens to call around asking for you."

"Well, thank fuck for that." He chuckled softly despite his mood, but then his eyes turned serious and searched mine.

In that moment, I felt like he was staring into my soul. But it was in the very best way, like his blue gaze had the power to fill me up with love.

"I never want to be without you," I whispered. "I want us. I *need* us."

"I do too, baby," he said and slid his hands up and down my arms. "Can we decide right here and now that whatever we do in terms of the future, we do it together?"

"Yes." I rubbed my nose against his. "And I really hope our future plans include living together. I've gotten used to you always being here. I don't think I could do the whole long-distance thing when it comes to you. It would be too hard to have to go days or weeks without seeing you."

"Of course they do." He smiled. "One day, you'll be my wife, and it would make zero fucking sense for us to be living anywhere else but together, baby."

My heart started pounding erratically in my chest at his words.

"Your wife?" I asked and he nodded.

"*My* wife." He pressed a kiss to my lips. "*Mine.*" His kiss turned deeper, and when my lips parted, he slipped his tongue inside my mouth to dance with mine.

I kissed him back with everything I had, and he slid his hands into my hair.

"I love you," he whispered against my lips. "I love you more than I knew it was even possible to love someone. And every day, that love keeps growing. You're my heart, Ivy. My whole fucking heart."

Tears pricked my eyes at his words. But it wasn't out of sadness. It was relief. It was joy. It was love. It was everything good. "I love you too."

He kissed me again, but this time, I felt his arousal grow harder between my thighs, and I moaned against his lips.

"I need you," he said. "I need to be inside of you, baby."

"Yes," I whimpered. He stood up with me in his arms, and I wrapped my legs around his waist.

He walked us toward the bed and softly laid me on the mattress. His impatient fingers made quick work of my pants and underwear before doing the same with his clothes. And then he moved his body on top of mine and slowly, oh so slowly, slid himself inside of me. Bare. Skin to skin. Pure fucking bliss.

Goose bumps and pleasure rolled up my spine, and a soft moan escaped my lips when he filled me.

Nose to nose, his blue gaze locked with mine, we just stared at one another while Levi gently rocked his hips, moving himself in and out at a soft, slow, intimate pace.

"Let me make love to you, baby," he said, and when I searched his eyes, I found his heart. "I want to spend the rest of the night inside of you."

I didn't have to think twice.

"Yes."

I needed this.

We needed this.

And it wasn't out of avoidance or to distract ourselves from the chaos that seemed to follow us around. It was out of pure need for one another. Out of deep, life-changing love for one another.

Tonight, I needed to be connected to him. I needed to feel him and love him and just be with him.

No distractions. Just us. Two people who simply loved one another more than anything else in the world.

CHAPTER
FIFTEEN

Levi

June 3rd, 2016

AWOKE WITH A START, BUT I COULDN'T QUITE UNDERSTAND WHAT HAD stirred me from my sleep. It took several blinks for me to open my tired eyes, but once I was able to make out the still-dark hotel room, I reached my arm out toward Ivy's side of the bed and came up empty-handed.

Where is she?

I sat up then and leaned toward the nightstand to switch on the light.

It was completely silent, until it wasn't.

A small gagging noise echoed from the bathroom inside our hotel suite, and that was followed up by several strong heaves, and after that, well, it was pretty easy to put two and two together.

Ivy was in the bathroom, and by the sounds of it, she was sicker than a dog.

"Ivy? You okay, baby?" I asked and slid off the bed and to my feet.

"I'm fine," she said, but her feeble voice said the opposite.

I rounded the bed and made my way toward the bathroom.

The door was shut, but once I opened it with a turn of the knob and a gentle shove of my hip, my eyes were assaulted by bright white light.

It only took a few moments for my vision to readjust, but once it did, I found Ivy sitting on the cool tile floor, her naked body clinging to the toilet like it was a life raft.

Her face was pale, and sweat droplets pebbled her forehead.

"Are you sick?" I asked, but she didn't have any time to answer.

She leaned forward with a weak groan and vomited into the toilet.

Yellow bile spewed out of her mouth, and her bare stomach kept contracting violently, forcing everything inside of her body up and out.

Quickly, I moved toward her and held her blond hair out of her face.

She tried to brush me away, moaning near incoherent words about not watching, but there was no way in hell I was leaving her alone like this.

Once she was finished, she sagged against the toilet, and her pale skin had morphed and she was white as a ghost. Tears dripped down her cheeks while droplets of sweat slid down her bare back.

"Baby, what's going on? You okay?" I asked and she groaned.

"I have no idea. I just woke up and had to pee, but while I was in the bathroom washing my hands, I started to get so nauseous. And then, next thing I knew, I was puking."

"Jesus," I muttered. "Do you think it's something you ate?"

"Well, if it was, that shouldn't be a problem now. There's literally nothing left."

I moved toward the sink and grabbed a fresh washcloth and held it under a spray of cold water before placing it on the back of Ivy's neck.

"Thank you," she said, and a little moan left her lips. "That's much better."

Eventually, she scooted away from the toilet until her back was pressed against the tile wall. "Okay… Thank everything…I think I'm actually starting to feel a lot better."

Understanding the general path of something like a stomach virus or food poisoning, I thought maybe that was wishful thinking, but I kept those thoughts to myself. The likelihood of more puking was the last thing she probably wanted to hear right now.

"Can I get you anything?" I asked, and she looked up at me with those big green eyes of hers and offered a little smile.

"Mind helping me up so I can brush my teeth and wash my face?"

"Like you even have to ask," I said, but instead of offering her a hand, I leaned down and slid my arms beneath her bent legs and behind her back and cradled her body against my chest.

"Jesus, Levi," she said through a few giggles as I lifted her up into the air, and I smiled.

God, it was a fucking relief to feel so light and full at the same time.

It'd been a rough stretch, both mentally and emotionally, and despite Ivy being sick, it was nice not to be thinking about difficult things like Camilla's death or my absent, shitty mother's hand in the movie *Cold*.

She'd tried to contact me through Ivy's manager, Mariah, but the law had already been laid down, and I outright refused to have any sort of contact with her.

Maybe some people would disagree, but I'd had enough pain at the hands of that woman, and I refused to open myself up to any more.

June Gatto wasn't a part of my life.

She may have been a scar from my past, but she sure as fuck wouldn't play any sort of part in my future.

"You can put me down now, you big lug," Ivy said with a giggle.

"All I needed was a hand. Pretty sure I could've handled the rest."

"I live to serve you, baby," I teased and smiled down at her.

"No, no, no," she said and covered her mouth with her hand. "I know that look. That look is bad fucking news, and I don't want that look from you until after I've brushed my damn teeth."

I grinned. "I have no idea what you're talking about."

She laughed at that. "Yeah, you do, you big fat liar."

I set her to her feet, and she playfully shoved an elbow into my stomach before moving to the bathroom sink and brushing her teeth.

Amazed at how quickly she appeared to be recovering from her puke session, I walked out of the bathroom and grabbed her a pair of underwear and one of my oversized white T-shirts she always loved to wear to bed.

But by the time I reached the bathroom, Ivy's mood had appeared to drift real fucking far away from feeling better and playful.

Eyes distant and mouth slack, she stared at herself in the mirror.

She looked a million miles away and seemed to have completely forgotten about the running sink water or the toothbrush in her hand.

My heart sank to my stomach.

"Baby?" I asked and moved directly behind her. "You feel sick again?"

She shook her head and opened and closed her mouth several times, but nothing came out. I felt like it took a million years before she pushed words out of her mouth.

"I...I think it's been two months," she whispered, and then she dropped her toothbrush into the sink. It fell with clang and started floating beneath the running water. She gasped and lifted her hand to cover her mouth. "Oh my God, it's definitely been at least two months, maybe more..."

I had no idea what she was talking about, but instantly, my mind went to Camilla.

It was the most obvious path.

"Two months? What are you talking about, Ivy?"

"My…my…my period," she whispered.

"What about your period?" I asked, but then my brain caught up with my words, and it was my turn to stare into the mirror.

"Levi…" She turned on her heels and stared up at me with shock raising her brow high on her forehead. "I…I think I might be pregnant."

Pregnant?

Ivy was pregnant?

No way.

No fucking way…*right?*

■

Stealthy ninja moves were the only way we managed a trip to the CVS up the street from the Beverly Wilshire Hotel at six in the morning.

Luckily, the last time Mariah had stopped by to chat with Ivy, she'd brought a bag full of disguises. Sunglasses, wigs, oversized hoodies, you name it and we had it.

And this morning, I'd gone the hat and hoodie route, while Ivy had decided to be a brunette.

Dazed and slightly confused by our current situation, the two of us had entered the pharmacy hand in hand, and after a good thirty minutes of walking aimlessly around the store, we'd left with a white plastic bag filled with pregnancy tests, Twizzlers, dill pickle Pringles, and a jug of SunnyD.

The food and drink choices were all Ivy.

By the time we'd gotten back to our hotel room, Ivy had eaten most of the snacks and drunk about half of the SunnyD.

And now, we waited.

Two minutes.

One hundred and twenty seconds until we'd find out our answer.

She'd peed on the test and left it in the bathroom while both of us pretty much paced the floor of the living room.

Jesus. I had no idea what to think.

I mean, Ivy could very well be pregnant. Which meant I would be a father.

And, let's face it, I hadn't had the best role models for parents.

My mother, well, she was a fucking stranger who had left when I was just a kid. And my dad had been an intolerant, money-hungry asshole from the day June Fox—*or I should say, June fucking Gatto*—had stepped out the front door of our house in Cold, until he took his very last breath.

My childhood had been a shitty one, filled with more pain than love.

More sadness than happy moments.

Mostly neglect and very little nurture.

How could I be a good father to a child with a childhood like that corroding my past?

Honestly, having a child with Ivy wasn't the scary part of this scenario for me.

I loved Ivy, and I knew she would be an amazing mother. I wanted to spend the rest of my life with her. Hell, when I'd picture our future, I'd sometimes see kids.

But that was different.

Those were daydreams.

That wasn't right now. That wasn't reality.

This was reality. This was real.

And this whole being a good dad thing had me on edge.

I didn't want to fuck up another human being the way my parents had done to me.

Every child deserved to grow up inside of a home filled with support and strong parental figures. A home filled with nothing but love.

Could I give that kind of home to a child?

With Ivy, you can.

Not to mention, the timing was all fucking wrong.

I feared it would be too much for Ivy to handle.

She'd just lost her sister. She'd just started to even allow herself to find moments of joy between the grief.

Would she be able to emotionally handle a pregnancy right now?

I wasn't sure, and it was probably that over everything that scared me the most.

I'd seen her suffer through so much, and I wasn't sure if my heart could bear seeing her feel misplaced guilt and sadness over being pregnant.

"I can't be pregnant...*right?*" she asked and yanked me from my thoughts. She stopped in the middle of the floor to meet my gaze, and both hands went to her hips. "I mean...what are the odds?" She questioned and then groaned and ran frustrated hands through her hair.

Considering I knew we'd had unprotected sex on more than one occasion, I wanted to tell her the odds might have been a little better than she thought. I mean, it seemed my brain turned fucking caveman when it came to Ivy and all rational thought left the fucking building, including ones that allowed for the forethought to put a goddamn condom on.

But I decided to keep my mouth shut. Ivy was too amped up with anxiety as it was, and in a matter of seconds, we'd know the results anyway.

Truth be told, I didn't even know what I wanted the result to be.

On one hand, I felt deep, all-consuming joy over the idea of having a baby with Ivy.

And on the other, well, I was anxious.

We had just barely started to gain our footing.

Ivy was slowly finding herself again.

We still had so many things to figure out. I mean, we were still living inside of a hotel room, for fuck's sake. This wasn't the most perfect timing for a baby.

"I'm scared, Levi," she whispered. "And I feel bad about being scared."

My heart ached like a son of a bitch inside of my chest.

"Baby, it's okay to be scared. It's okay to feel whatever it is you're feeling right now."

I sure as fuck was all over the place with my thoughts and emotions.

But I refused to tell her that right now.

I just wanted and needed to stay calm for her.

The alarm she had set on her phone went off and startled us both.

Time's up.

We stared at one another for a long moment.

"It's time," she whispered, and instantly, I knew. I had to do something before we stepped inside that bathroom to find out our fate.

"Hold on," I said and moved toward her. She opened her mouth to question what I was doing, but I used that opportunity to pull her body close to mine and press my mouth to hers.

I kissed her. Long, deep, and filled with all of the love in the world, I kissed Ivy with everything I had.

Eventually, I slowed the kiss back down and pulled away, but for the longest moment, I just let my lips linger against hers. "I love you," I whispered, and I felt her quick intake of breath. "I know this is scary right now, especially considering the timing, but just know that I love you, Ivy, and I'm here and I'm not going anywhere."

She looked up at me, and the emotion shining in her eyes slayed me.

"You mean that?" she whispered, and I nodded.

"Of course I do," I said and wiped away her tears with my thumbs. "You're my whole fucking world, baby."

"You're mine too," she said softly, and my heart pounded like a drum inside my chest.

"Well, then, no matter what happens, it'll be okay."

She nodded and repeated my words. "No matter what happens, it'll be okay."

I grabbed her hand and held it within mine. "Ready?"

"As I'll ever be, I guess," she said through a tight laugh, and I smiled down at her before leading her into the bathroom.

"You check," she squeaked out the instant we stepped foot onto the cool white tile. "You check first and then tell me what it says."

With her hand still in mine, I pulled the pregnancy test off the edge of the bathtub and read the result.

Pregnant.

My heart felt like an elevator gone rogue, diving through my stomach, down my legs, and hitting my feet.

Ivy was pregnant.

Holy. Shit.

"Well…" She paused, and the nerves were evident in her voice. "What does it say?"

I set the pregnancy test back down and pulled Ivy straight into my arms and kissed her. "Looks like we're going to have a baby," I whispered against her lips.

"I'm pregnant?" she asked, and tears filled her eyes. "We're going to have a baby?"

"Yeah, baby." I couldn't not smile. This was good news. This was amazing news. Surprise or not, this was something that urged joy into my heart. "We're going to have a baby."

Her hand abruptly reached up to cover her mouth, and she stepped away from me to check the results for herself.

With shaky hands, she picked up the pregnancy test and stared down at the result window.

She glanced up at me, then back down at the test, until finally, her gaze landed back to mine where it stayed. "Oh my God," she whispered. "I'm pregnant. We're pregnant."

"We are." I nodded, and my vision fogged with a sheen of happy emotion.

But I held my tears back and searched Ivy's face closely.

I watched and waited.

I wasn't sure how she was going to react.

I wasn't sure what she was thinking.

I wasn't sure about anything except that I loved her and the baby growing inside of her belly.

Ivy moved toward the bathroom mirror and pulled up her shirt to reveal the soft, toned skin of her belly. "There's a baby growing inside of there, Levi," she whispered. "Right now. A teeny tiny baby is in there."

I stood behind her and wrapped my arms around her waist and placed my hand over hers. "*Our* teeny tiny baby."

A few tears spilled from her cheeks.

"I just… I can't believe it…" She paused, and her voice shook with emotion.

And then she smiled, and it lit up my whole damn world.

A deep breath escaped my lungs, and I felt the worry and concern release from my shoulders.

She tilted her head to look up at me. "Our baby."

CHAPTER
SIXTEEN

Ivy

June 4th, 2016

"**Y**OU OKAY?" LEVI ASKED AND I SHRUGGED.

Considering that any minute the obstetrician Mariah had contacted for me would be here, I sure as shit was trying to be okay.

I wouldn't say it was working, But I was trying like hell.

"Yeah...just a little nervous," I whispered, and he wrapped an arm around my shoulder and pulled me closer to his side.

We were sitting on the couch in the small living room of our hotel room, which lately, had turned into our home away from home.

Truthfully, I was growing tired of it. I missed sleeping in my own bed.

I missed my house in Beverly Hills.

Initially, I'd been avoiding going home because my house had been Camilla's house too, and it was too difficult to be there.

But now, it was more related to the paparazzi waiting outside of my property, ready to snap any photos they could get their lens on.

Inside the hotel, we had some privacy. We had more control.

Not only because of our security staff, but the hotel had their own as well.

The front entrance of the establishment was always monitored by guards. And anytime we left the premises, we were able to go through the back, staff-only entrance. By the time paparazzi realized we were on the move, we were already fifteen minutes away.

Sure, they still always managed to catch up with us at some point, but at least it all felt a lot more manageable.

Still, though, it was a fucking hotel room and a poor excuse for a home.

But right now, our current living arrangements were the very last thing on my mind.

Reruns of *Curb Your Enthusiasm* played on the television, but I had no idea what Larry David or Ted Danson was saying.

I couldn't focus on anything but my racing thoughts.

Yesterday, I'd found out I was pregnant.

Twenty-four hours ago, I'd gone from a woman who was trying to hold it all together while grieving the death of her sister, to a woman who was pregnant and trying to hold it all together while grieving the death of her sister.

I had so many thoughts, so many fucking emotions filling me up that I didn't know what or how to feel.

I was definitely anxious.

I mean, was I ready to be a mom? Was I ready to be responsible for another human being? Was the timing of this pregnancy going to be too hard for me to deal with emotionally? My heart was still so vulnerable, so fragile since I'd lost my sister.

But, deep down, I was also excited.

Levi and I were going to have a baby. A little person that we created, albeit completely accidentally, but still created all the same.

And it was actually those emotions that were the hardest.

They made me feel guilty.

They filled me up with so much joy, and then that joy turned into feeling bad about being this happy. I wasn't sure if I was allowed to be this happy when I didn't have Camilla.

My sister wasn't here.

I couldn't share the news with her.

I couldn't watch and hear her reaction when I told her I was pregnant.

I couldn't tell her all of my hopes and fears.

She was gone, and it felt like there would always be a part of me that would remain a little bit lost without her.

Sadness and guilt and grief hit me all at once, and I blinked against the emotion that threatened to spill out from my eyes.

God, I miss Camilla.

Sometimes, at random times during the day, I'd see or hear or think about something that would remind me of her, and it would make my heart ache so badly.

Levi pulled me tighter to his side and kissed the side of my forehead. "It's going to be okay, baby," he whispered. "And just remember, whatever you're feeling right now, it's okay. You're allowed to feel what you feel. If you're happy, be happy. If you're sad, be sad. If you're both, be both. Just know I'm here."

Sometimes, I wondered if he could read my mind. We were so attuned to one another it was uncanny, and still, it took me by surprise.

I turned to look at him, and when I locked my gaze with his eyes, they were endless blue oceans of nothing but love and comfort and solace. Levi's eyes were like my own little slice of serenity inside a world of chaos.

He'd become my savior.

The man I could always rely on.

Thank God, thank everything, for him.

"Thank you," I whispered.

"For what?" he asked and quirked a curious brow.

"For saying exactly what I needed you to say right now."

He responded with a gentle kiss to my mouth, and I sighed against his soft lips.

But I only had mere moments to savor the comfort he provided because a minute or two later, a few soft knocks echoed off the front door.

I looked at Levi, and he looked at me.

"I guess it's time, huh?"

"Yeah, baby," he said and stood to his feet. "It's time," he called over his shoulder as he went to the door.

He greeted the doctor in the entry, and I eventually found the strength to get off the couch and meet the woman who would be confirming my pregnancy.

"Hi," I said and held out my hand once the doctor stepped into the small living room area with a large black wheeling suitcase rolling behind her. "I'm Ivy Stone."

She smiled and shook my hand. "It's so nice to meet you, Ivy. I'm Dr. Macintosh."

The doctor was all business in a black pantsuit and white silk blouse. Her jet-black hair was pulled up into a chignon, and her makeup was pretty much impeccable. She was very pretty, and her brown eyes told me she was also very honest and sweet.

You could tell so much from someone's eyes. When I'd first met Levi, I'd known those midnight-blue eyes had held secrets and pain. But I'd also known there was more to him. So much more and I had been desperate to find it.

"Thank you for coming on such short notice, and to our hotel room, at that," Levi said, and Dr. Macintosh smiled.

"Of course," she responded with a nod. "I understand the need for privacy. Especially for the two of you right now." She looked at me, and her brown eyes turned soft. "And, Ivy, I'd like to offer my heartfelt condolences. I'm so sorry about the loss of your sister."

"Thank you. That means a lot."

Somehow, someway, hearing those kinds of words got easier.

Rather than pain and irritation, I just felt accepting and maybe even a little thankful for them.

"Well, are you ready to get started?" she asked, and I nodded.

"Would it be best to do this in the bedroom or...?"

"The bedroom will work just fine," she answered, and I led the way while Levi and the doctor followed.

Once we stepped inside, she got right down to business, and he sat down in one of the chairs near the large window.

Dr. Macintosh started unpacking her black suitcase with all kinds of medical equipment, and I swallowed hard against the anxiety threatening to claw its way out of my chest and up my throat.

"So, you took a pregnancy test yesterday, and it was positive?" she asked, and for lack of anything better to do, I sat down on the edge of the bed while she finished getting set up.

"Yes."

"And when was your last period?"

"Um..." I worried my lip with my teeth. "I think it's been two months, but honestly, I'm not very sure."

"And were you on any type of birth control?"

"Well, I was on the pill, but I had to go off of it several months ago because of the side effects. We used condoms...sometimes...but I hadn't figured out a replacement hormonal method yet."

Dr. Macintosh nodded like she understood—like she understood *precisely* how I'd gotten pregnant. Sex wasn't like the lottery. Unless Levi was shooting blanks, unprotected sex meant a hell of a lot bigger than a one in fourteen million chance of getting pregnant. "And this is your first pregnancy, correct?"

"Correct."

"Okay, Ivy," she instructed and set a paper gown on the bed, near my hip. "I want you to go into the bathroom and take off your clothes, bra and underwear included, and put this gown on. And while you're doing that, I'll put a plastic drape on the bed."

I did as I was told, and five minutes later, I was lying on our hotel room bed while Dr. Macintosh started her exam.

"Any nausea or vomiting?" she asked and I nodded.

"Definitely nausea and a little bit of vomiting too."

"Breast tenderness?"

"Yes."

"Okay, good," she said, and I didn't necessarily agree those were good things, but I just went with it. "Now, I'm going to do a quick vaginal exam on you before we do an ultrasound."

"Okay," I said quietly and looked to the side to find Levi staring over at me. I grimaced a little as she started to examine me, more from the coldness of the lubricant she had used than anything else, but also just the fact that some woman I'd met all of twenty minutes ago currently had her hand all up inside my vagina.

I mean, I was probably being a little dramatic, but this wasn't exactly a heavenly, feel-good, kind of moment.

Levi stood up from his chair and moved over to the bed to sit beside me. He reached out and clasped my hand in his, gently running his thumbs over my skin in soothing circles.

"Your cervix is definitely closed," Dr. Macintosh said.

"Is that good?" I asked and she smiled.

"When it comes to a pregnancy, yes, it's a good thing," she answered and finished up the vaginal exam.

She stood up from the bed and slipped off her latex gloves before stepping into the bathroom to wash her hands for a brief moment.

"Now, I'm going to do a vaginal ultrasound. It is similar to the vaginal exam I just did, only this time, I'm going to insert this probe inside of you so that I can see inside your uterus." She held up the probe, and my eyes went a little wide.

"Is it going to hurt?"

She shook her head. "It's not painful. If anything, you'll just feel some pressure."

I took a deep breath and prepared myself for another invasion of my most personal space.

Once she set up the portable ultrasound machine on the night-stand, she slipped on another pair of latex gloves and proceeded to gently slide the large probe inside of me.

Pressure? *Oh my.* It was there. Oh boy, was it there.

She moved the probe around, and I cringed a little at the increased force.

"Oh wow," she said as she looked at the screen.

Oh wow? What does that mean?

"Does everything look okay?" I asked, and Levi sat up straight, worry revealing itself in his blue eyes.

"Yes, but I have some news for you," Dr. Macintosh said and looked at me and then at Levi.

My heart dropped out of my body.

Oh God, was the test wrong?

Had I taken a faulty test, and I wasn't even pregnant?

"I'm not pregnant?" The words just flew from my lips, and Dr. Macintosh smiled.

"You are definitely pregnant," she said, and I breathed a sigh of relief. "And from the looks of it, you're going to have twins."

Oh, thank God.

Wait…what?

"Hold on…what did you say?" I damn near shouted. "What do you mean twins?"

"Well…" she said and paused for a brief moment to turn a knob on the ultrasound machine. "Do you hear that?" she asked, and a soft and speedy *bum-bum-bum* filled my ears.

"Yes."

"That's your baby's heartbeat. And this," she said and moved the probe a little. "Well, this is your other baby's heartbeat."

"Two heartbeats?" Levi questioned with wide-as-saucer eyes.

"Yep." She smiled. "Two heartbeats. Two babies."

Two babies? As in, two babies growing inside of me? At the same freaking time?

"Congratulations, Levi and Ivy. It looks like you're nine, maybe even ten weeks pregnant with twins."

I looked at Levi, and his shocked blue gaze locked with mine.

"Twins?" I mouthed, and he blinked several times, but then after a few seconds, a small, happy little smile crested his lips.

"We sure as fuck don't do anything half-assed, do we?" he asked, voice equal parts shocked and amused.

My eyes wide, I couldn't stop a giggle from escaping my lips.

"Apparently not."

CHAPTER
SEVENTEEN

Levi

July 8th, 2016

IVY AND I HAD BEEN BACK IN COLD, MONTANA FOR TWO DAYS, AND the instant our plane had landed, I felt like we'd been going nonstop.

It was a much-needed trip, though.

I'd needed to give Chief Pulse my official notice. Sure, I could have done it over the phone, but it was something I wanted to do in person. He'd been like a father to me, and I had to tell him the news that I'd be permanently staying with Ivy on the West Coast face-to-face.

I'd needed to make sure things were running smoothly at Ruby Jane's.

I'd wanted to catch up with all of the important people that were a huge part of my life in Cold. Jeremy and Liza and the girls, Sam, Mary, and so many others. It was a surprisingly long list for a guy who had spent the better part of the past nearly seven years striving to avoid anything that made him feel too much.

And I'd needed to make sure the seventeen-year-old kid I'd hired to watch over my house and keep my yard up to snuff was doing what he should.

Not to mention, I needed to figure out what in the fuck I was going to do with this big-ass house since I wouldn't be living in Montana anymore.

It felt weird selling it, and I sure as fuck didn't need the money from it, but it also felt stupid for it to stay empty.

Instantly, I thought about Jeremy and his family.

I knew Liza loved her little house on the outskirts of town, but I also knew they were running out of space. Surely, Jeremy would put up a fight, but I'd have to find a way to convince him. Not to mention, they could sell their house, and instead of having to put the profit toward a new mortgage, they could just put that money away for the girls' college fund.

I made a mental note to put that on my to-do list before we left.

And then I made a mental note to block out three or more spots on the to-do list at the least. It was going to be a hard sell, and I suspected it wouldn't be the kind of thing that went quickly. Jeremy was the type of guy who liked to work for everything he got, but I'd just have to find a way to make him think he was doing me a favor more than anything else.

Once I slipped on my boots, I checked the time and realized we needed to haul ass if we wanted to be at Sam's place by noon.

"You ready, baby?" I called toward the bathroom. I stepped over the threshold of the master en suite and found Ivy standing inside my bathroom, fidgeting with her hair and frowning.

"Once I figure out something to do with my hair," she said and picked up a brush to run it through her still blond locks. "Rat's nests have looked better than this mess on my head."

"You're crazy, baby. You look incredibly gorgeous."

She rolled her eyes. "I appreciate the compliment, but you don't understand because you're a man."

I chuckled at that. "What's me being a man have to do with how your hair looks?"

"Because men don't get the kind of maintenance that is required to a be girl. Your daily routine consists of brushing your teeth and taking a fucking shower. And that's literally it."

"Sometimes I have to shave."

"Ohh man. Alert the freaking media," she said with a sarcastic little grin.

"And sometimes I have to watch you change your outfit fifteen times," I teased, and her face morphed into a glare. "That is also a large part of my routine."

She turned those fiery green eyes away from the mirror and onto me. "Don't start with me today, Fox," she said and pointed her brush at my face. "I spent the first two hours of my morning puking. And then another hour trying to force breakfast down my throat despite feeling like a motion-sick sailor in a hurricane."

Nearly four months pregnant with identical twins and Ivy was deeply in the trenches of what most would call morning sickness. Although, lately, it appeared it was all-day sickness.

She puked more than a hungover frat kid.

I held up both hands and relinquished the unwinnable battle that was dealing with a hormonal, pregnant Ivy. She lived her life on a hair trigger these days, and ironically, today, the trigger seemed to be hair. "Listen, you take all the time you need. I'll give Sam a call and let him know we're running a little late."

"What time is it?"

"Quarter till noon."

"We're supposed to be there at noon!" she exclaimed, and I wanted to point out that was exactly why I was in here trying to get her to stop worrying about her hair, but I preferred to keep my balls intact, thank you very much.

So, instead, I just stared back at her with the most neutral expression I could force on to my face. "Well, I'm sure Sam will understand. Do you want me to tell him we'll be there at 12:30?"

She sighed, tossing her hair into a high ponytail with quick hands, her long blond locks hanging down her back in gorgeous waves.

How this woman could ever think she was anything less than beautiful was beyond me.

"All right," she said and tossed the brush back onto the counter. "I guess this will just have to do. I don't want to make Sam wait any longer."

She strode out of the bathroom and slipped on little black flats.

I followed her lead out of the bedroom and into the living room, and as I watched her grab her purse from the kitchen counter, I marveled at the fact that she had the teeniest hint of a baby belly showing beneath her tank top.

Just the idea of it made me grin, and I couldn't stop myself from stepping toward her and placing my hand on her belly.

"W-what are you doing?" She looked up at me, eyes narrowed in confusion, but I just smiled down at her like she was my whole fucking world.

Because, God, Ivy Stone was my whole fucking world.

We'd been through so fucking much.

We'd had to deal with so much.

But one constant had always remained—I loved this woman madly.

The fact that she was pregnant with my kids filled me up with so much joy, sometimes it felt like my heart was going to explode out of my chest.

I squatted down, and with both hands on her barely showing belly, I pressed my lips against it. "Hi, babies," I whispered and stared up at Ivy. "I hope you're nice and cozy in there."

The frustrated tension of her brow lifted, and she gazed down at me in awe.

One last kiss to her belly and I stood to my feet. "Ready?"

She stepped up on her tippy-toes and pressed her lips to the corner of my mouth. "I love you, you swoony fucking charmer, you. I'm sorry for my bitchy outburst earlier. I'd like to say it won't happen again, but that would probably be a lie."

I chuckled at that and wrapped my arm around her shoulders. "Love you too, baby."

We walked out of my house and hopped into the truck. And it didn't take long before we were on the main road, driving through the familiar roads of Cold, Montana.

The town looked so damn small in comparison to the LA city-scape I'd become accustomed to over the past few months.

It was cozy and homey, and I knew if I'd miss anything, it would be the way a small town like Cold could make you feel. Welcoming and warm and laid-back, it was the polar opposite of LA.

Where life sped by at a one-hundred-miles-an-hour pace there, in Cold, the days drifted and the hours waned, and no one appeared to be in a hurry to do anything.

It was refreshing.

But after a while, I knew it held the possibility to make some people feel restless.

June Fox turned June Gatto was a prime example of that. I didn't want Ivy Stone to be another.

Cold hadn't been enough for my mom. She'd wanted more. And apparently, she'd needed more so much she was willing to leave her child behind.

Despite her efforts, I'd yet to have any contact with my mother since that day Ivy and I had stepped into her office.

And I didn't regret it.

For me, I had all of the closure I needed when I found out she'd written the screenplay for a movie about one of the worst things to ever happen in my life.

Some people might have thought I was cutting myself short, that I was giving up on the possibility of having a relationship with her, but I knew my limits. And when it came to my mom, I'd more reached them. I'd managed just fine without her for most of my life, and I sure as fuck didn't need her now.

But that didn't mean I couldn't learn from the lessons she'd taught. When it came to what Ivy wanted to do, I had to be open to the possibility that staying in Cold wasn't what would make her happy. We'd agreed to head back to LA for now, but ultimately, I hoped we'd compromise on something a little less chaotic.

After driving through the city and onto the back roads, I turned into Sam's driveway, and Ivy bounced excitedly in the passenger seat.

The instant my truck slowed to a stop, Sam's smiling figure came striding out of the front door. He glowed with excitement as he walked over to the truck and opened Ivy's door.

"Ivy girl," Sam greeted with a big ole grin. "Well, aren't you a sight for sore eyes. You're practically glowing, sweetheart. God, it's so good to see you." He wrapped her up in a warm hug, and I cut the engine and slid out of the driver's seat.

When I rounded the truck and met them on the other side, the old man's kind eyes turned to me.

He didn't hold back, also pulling me into a tight hug and patting my back a few times with a strong hand. "Good to see you, son," he said and I smiled.

"Good to see you too."

"Well, come on inside," he said and gestured us toward the front door. "I've got a pot of chili ready."

We followed his lead, and the instant we stepped inside the front door, the delicious aroma of home-cooked chili filled my nose.

Damn, it'd been a long while since I'd had some of Sam's famous chili.

My stomach growled in excitement at the mere thought of it.

But my eagerness over food turned to concern when I looked over at Ivy to find her eyes wide and lips clenched tightly together.

Her throat bobbed harshly as she swallowed a few times.

And then, quick as a whip, she lifted her hand to her mouth and ran in the direction of the bathroom.

Oh, fuck.

Morning sickness and chili were apparently not a good mix.

"Ivy?" Sam questioned with big eyes, but Ivy was long gone, inside his bathroom down the hall. "Is she okay?" he asked.

I hesitated underneath his curious stare.

We hadn't told him the big news yet.

Hell, we hadn't told anyone but Ivy's parents. They'd been beyond elated when we'd shown them the ultrasound pictures over dinner at their house two weeks ago.

Helen had hopped up from her seat with tears in her eyes and hugged Ivy so tightly it made me grin from ear to ear. And Dave had immediately followed her lead, hugging both of his girls in his arms as the three of them verbalized their joy through I love yous and congratulations.

It had been a beautiful moment.

And I didn't want to rob Ivy of experiencing that same kind of moment with Sam.

So, I did my best to brush off his concern.

"Uh, yeah," I muttered. "She was feeling a little unwell today. I'll go check to see if she's all right."

Sam stared back at me with puzzlement in his eyes, but I just turned on my heels and went to check on Ivy. By the time I reached the bathroom door, she was already heaving this morning's breakfast into the toilet.

"You okay?" I asked her on a whisper as I stepped inside.

She nodded but then heaved once more.

But eventually, she made a miraculous recovery, which I'd learned was common with morning sickness, and hopped back to her feet.

She stopped at the sink to splash some cold water onto her face and swish the bile out of her mouth, but as quick as it hit her, she was completely over it.

She reached into her purse and popped a Tic Tac into her mouth. "I think it was just the smell of chili. My stomach wasn't expecting it."

"You going to be okay to stay inside the house?"

She nodded. "Yeah, I think so."

"Well, just let me know if that changes, okay?"

She nodded again, and we made our way back into the living room.

Grandpa Sam stood at the mouth of the hallway, his hands crossed over his chest.

"All right," he said, and both Ivy and I stopped in front of him. "What's going on?"

"What do you mean, Sam?" Ivy asked, and he glanced down at her belly before meeting her eyes again.

"Glowing like the sun...running to the bathroom to puke... I might be an old man, but I'm still quick as a whip, darlin'," he said, and Ivy burst into laughter.

"You're so ornery sometimes, I swear," she said through a few giggles. "And just so you know, we were going to tell you, but apparently, you have zero patience."

His brow rose up in surprise. "So, it's true?" he asked and looked back and forth between us. "You're pregnant?"

Ivy and I both smiled at each other for a brief moment, and then she broke our gaze to meet Sam's excited eyes again. "I'm almost four months along," she said, and her hand instinctually reached up to gently rest on her tiny little belly.

"Four months along?" he questioned and then clapped his hands. "Well, I'll be damned! If that ain't the best news I've heard in a long, long time!" He stepped forward and wrapped both of us up in a big ole bear hug. "Congratulations, you two. I couldn't be any happier about this news."

"Well..." Ivy's smile grew wide and amused. "There's one more thing, actually..."

He quirked a brow. "One more thing?"

"Uh-huh," she said and nodded. "We're having twins."

"*Twins?*" His jaw damn near hit the floor. "*Two* babies?" he asked and held up two fingers in the air.

"Yep," I said and placed my hand on Ivy's belly. "There's two little babies in there."

Sam clapped his hands again. "Well, talk about some good news. I can't wait to tell Mary. She will be so happy."

It was moments like these, hearing Sam, Grace's grandfather, chatter on excitedly about Ivy's pregnancy that I realized just how far we'd come.

Life had thrown us some serious punches. Some life-altering obstacles.

And there were days where it almost felt like too much to handle.

But life had also given us this.

These special moments.

These amazing people.

This sometimes chaotic and messy, but always beautiful, life together.

We were blessed.

Even after all of the pain we'd suffered through. Even though we still had demons of our past that really gave us hell some days. Even despite all of that, we were lucky.

Wherever we decided to live, I knew I'd miss Cold. Most of all, I'd miss seeing all of the people inside this small town that had shaped my life, but none of them was the center of my world anymore.

The woman of my dreams and the babies in her belly were.

I was ready to start my life with Ivy.

With her by my side, wherever we were, whatever we were doing, I was home.

BREAKING NEWS: Ivy Stone is Pregnant!

July 20th, 2016

As of late, Ivy Stone's life has been a roller coaster ride of ups and downs, and an inside source has revealed the biggest news yet.

Buckle up, folks! Because things are about to get insanely surprising!

Ivy Stone and baby daddy Levi Fox were spotted leaving the back entrance of her OB/GYN's office, and a top-secret source inside the medical practice revealed that not only is Ivy Stone pregnant, but she is going to have twins!

Talk about a big surprise!

There has been no news on the sex of the babies or if Levi Fox and Ivy Stone plan to take the next big step in their relationship and get married, but everyone here at Celebrity Weekly is losing their minds over this amazing news!

Consider us officially on #StoxBabyWatch!

CHAPTER
EIGHTEEN

Ivy

July 30th, 2016

I SIGHED AS I SAT ON THE COUCH BASICALLY TWIDDLING MY FREAKING thumbs and not having a clue what to do with myself. For the last fifteen minutes, I'd been doing this, and still, I had no solution for my restlessness.

Luckily, my phone pinged with a text message, and I snagged it off the coffee table to find a text from my mom.

Mom: How are you feeling today, sweetheart?

I smiled as I typed out a response.

Me: I'm doing pretty good. Still dealing with some nausea in the morning, but no puking, so that's a big freaking win in my book.

Mom: That's great news. God, I can remember being sick as a dog when I was pregnant with you and Cami. It was miserable for practically my entire pregnancy.

Me: I didn't know that.

Mom: Oh, yeah. Hell had taken up residence in my throat during that pregnancy.

Me: LOL

Mom: But it was all worth it in the end. ☺ You know, I had a dream about Camilla last night.

Me: Really? What happened?

Mom: We were sitting on my bed just talking about you and your pregnancy. She was excited about the babies and said she thinks you're going to have girls.

Simultaneously, my heart warmed and ached as I read the message.

It was all so bittersweet.

I was beyond ecstatic about this pregnancy, but I was also sad my sister wasn't here to meet her nieces or nephews.

Which I'd decided to wait until the babies were born to find out what we were having. I wasn't normally the biggest fan of surprises, but for this, I was one hundred percent invested in waiting. For the first time in my life, I *wanted* to be surprised.

Maybe, deep down, I wanted this surprise because I knew it wouldn't end in tragedy.

No matter if our babies were boys or girls, it would be the surprise of a lifetime.

With my fingers to my phone, I typed out a message.

Me: Your dream makes my heart happy and a little sad at the same time. Mostly happy, though.

FOX

Mom: I felt the same way about it when I woke up this morning.

Me: I just wish my babies could have met their awesome aunt.

Mom: At least we can tell them about her.

Me: Yes. ☺ And show them pictures and videos and pretty much anything else I can think of. Even though she's not here physically, to me, she'll always be here in spirit. Cami is a part of me. Always and forever.

Mom: I love everything about this, Ivy. So much.

Me: Me too, Mom. Me too.

Mom: Okay, sweetheart, well, your dad and I have some errands to run. I just wanted to check in with you, but I'll call you tomorrow. Love you, sweetheart.

Me: Love you too, Mom.

Smiling to myself, I set my phone down on the coffee table and stood up.

But when I got to my feet, I realized I had nowhere to go.

Nowhere to be.

I was stuck here...inside this freaking house.

Restlessness back in full force, the familiar tinglings of annoyance started to filter into my veins, and the happiness high from chatting with my mom dropped like a rock.

God, I just wanted to get out of this house.

I wanted to breathe in the fresh air.

I wanted to take a walk with Levi and enjoy the California sun.

But ever since we'd left the hotel and tried to settle down in my house in Beverly Hills, I'd felt like a prisoner inside of my own home.

News had broken about my pregnancy, and the media firestorm had only grown.

They were hungry for every little detail.

They wanted to know about my pregnancy.

They wanted photos of my ever-growing belly.

They wanted to insert themselves as much as they could into our lives.

I wasn't new to what life was like when you were in the public eye, and a lot of things I understood and had no issues handling, but this was another level. An intolerable, chaotic, irritating level that made me hesitant to even leave my house.

Levi had added another security guy to our team, bringing the ridiculous total to *five*, but it just didn't matter.

We were in the Hollywood stronghold, where paparazzi were everywhere, waiting and watching in the wings, and it was damn near impossible to do anything without them on our asses, shoving their lenses in our faces and shouting intrusive questions about our lives.

Once we'd gotten home from our trip to Cold a few weeks ago, I thought moving back in to my house would be a step in the right direction. I thought it would be good for me to be surrounded by memories of Cami. And I thought we'd find peace being able to live out of a closet versus a suitcase, but my assumptions had been entirely incorrect on the latter.

I paced the hardwood floor of my entryway before turning in the opposite direction and heading out onto the back terrace. The pool shimmered and shone and looked so inviting, but nearly five months along with twins and I was starting to feel too damn pregnant to float around in the water like a beached whale.

I sat down on the edge of the pool and dangled my bare feet in the warm water. Leaning back on my elbows, I shut my eyes and let the sun wash over my face.

It was in these moments of rest that I realized just how tired I really was.

I'd spent the earlier part of the day chatting with my agent, Jason, about a script he'd sent over. It was a thriller about a CIA agent who goes rogue because she's been framed for a murder she didn't commit.

It had intrigued me from the start, and it was the first time since my sister had passed that I was actually considering taking on a new project.

And if the director could wait to shoot it until next year, I'd most likely be the actress playing the lead role.

It was truly ironic how a movie I didn't even want to see released had essentially taken my career to a point where I was in high demand for dozens of roles. Directors didn't even ask for me to audition.

Cold was well down its path toward its big debut to the public. The studio had even started revealing it to movie critics and the like, and the overwhelming opinion was that it would be one of the best movies of the year.

I both loved and hated it.

I was over the moon that I'd done Grace justice. That all of the hard work and struggle I'd gone through to bring her to life on screen hadn't been for naught.

But I still despised that a movie that had ended in my sister's death was going to be shown to the world, and I didn't have a fucking say in the matter.

The terrace door opened and shut, and I glanced over my shoulder to see Levi walking toward me. "What are you doing out here?"

"Just trying to get some fresh air," I said and squinted up at him.

"How was your meeting with Hugo?"

A couple of weeks ago, Hugo Roman had contacted Levi directly about a cop drama he was directing that he wanted Levi's expertise on.

Levi had been shocked to the say the least, but eventually, he'd agreed to a meeting.

"It went really well." He smiled, slipped off his shoes and socks and rolled up the legs of his jeans before sitting down beside me and placing his feet in the water. "We talked about the script, and I didn't know this, but Robert De Niro has been cast to play the police chief."

"Hot damn, De Niro?" I asked and grinned. "Sounds like you're about to go all Hollywood, Mr. Fox."

"I'm not going all Hollywood, smartass." He reached into the pool and flicked a few drops of water in my direction, and I laughed. "But I think, in terms of this film, there's definitely something I can bring to the table. So, I'll probably do it. Plus, Hugo is adamant. Apparently, I made an impression on him when I was on set for Cold."

"Well, you certainly made an impression on me when you were there," I said and smiled over at him. "I mean, at first, I pretty much hated you. But now? Look at me. I'm all knocked up with your babies. You certainly have a way of leaving your mark."

He chuckled at that and reached out to place a wet hand to my belly. The water soaked through my tank top, but I didn't mind. It was nearly ninety degrees outside. The cooldown was much appreciated. "How are my babies doing today?"

"Good and very busy kicking my rib cage."

"And how's their beautiful momma?"

"A little bit stressed."

He quirked a brow. "Stressed? What about?"

I sighed. "I thought things would be easier once we moved out of the hotel and into the house, but they're not, Levi. The media, the fucking paparazzi, right now, it's just too damn intolerable. I feel like I can't even walk outside without someone taking pictures and shouting questions at me. Like, I'm literally having insanely weird dreams about delivering the babies, and the doctor ends up being a journalist taking pictures of my vagina."

He barked out a laugh. "That's fucking terrifying."

"I know, right?" I responded through a soft laugh. "But...I don't know... I think maybe LA isn't the best place for us to be right now."

"You want to move out of LA?"

"Maybe?" I shrugged. "I mean, would you be okay with that?"

"Baby," he said, and his gaze turned earnest. "I want you to be happy and feel at peace in our home. And if you're not happy here, then I say we start shopping around and see if we can find a little less-busy place to settle down."

"Really?" I questioned. "You'd move? Just like that? *Again?*"

"Of course I would," he answered. "A house is just a fucking house, baby. You're my home."

I damn near swooned at his words.

"Sometimes, Levi Fox, you really do say some swoony shit." I leaned over to press a kiss to his lips. "Which is one of about a million reasons why I love you very much."

He grinned. "A million, huh? That's a lot."

"And the more I think about it, the more I'm certain on this whole moving thing," I answered honestly, ignoring his expedition for more compliments. "Do you mind if I contact some Realtors?"

"Not at all," he said and stood to his feet. "It's your world, baby. I'm just thankful you let me live in it."

Fucking hell. Levi Fox was a man of many talents, but this last one was a surprise.

He had an uncanny ability, when it came to me, to suck up.

Ivy Stone Is on the Move!

August 3rd, 2016

It appears that Ivy Stone is now in the market for a new house, and our inside source revealed she is adamant about moving away from the hectic LA lifestyle.

She has been spotted looking at homes in various locations on the West Coast, including smaller towns in Washington and Oregon, over the past few weeks, and it appears she won't be the only one living in her new home.

Her baby daddy and boyfriend Levi Fox has been with her every step of the way.

The pair has been thick as thieves ever since their romance started when Ivy was filming in the small town of Cold, Montana, where Levi Fox was not only a police officer inside the city's department, but also the real-life officer the movie *Cold* was based on.

Between Ivy's pregnancy and house shopping, we're all wondering if an engagement is the next big step for the Hollywood starlet.

Everyone at *CELEB NEWSIES* has their fingers and toes crossed that an Ivy Stone and Levi Fox wedding will be the next big news!

We'll keep our eyes on the mail for our invitation!

CHAPTER
NINETEEN

Levi

September 3rd, 2016

J UST AS I'D HOPED, WE'D MET IN THE MIDDLE. HALFWAY BETWEEN our respective homes in Montana and California, Ivy and I had settled on a place in Southern Oregon. It was off the grid and just enough distance from the hustle and bustle of LA and the painful memories that lay within Cold. We'd found our own little slice of secluded heaven with a gated entrance, a state-of-the-art security system, and our vetted security team keeping us safe.

Ivy had been campaigning for Oregon from the very start of our home search.

She'd been convinced I'd love the state and the people.

"Oregonians are like Canadians, Levi," she'd said. *"Impossibly nice and they wear sandals with wool socks. There isn't a person in the world who can wear wool socks and not be happy."*

California girl at heart, Ivy hadn't really experienced a bad winter in Cold, Montana. And trust me, even with wool socks on, Chief Pulse wasn't impossibly nice or happy.

But none of it really mattered. Although Ivy had felt she'd needed to convince me on Oregon, I would have gone any-fucking-where she wanted.

A house, whatever state it was in, was just a fucking place to put our stuff.

But my home? Well, that was all Ivy.

Wherever she was, that was exactly where I needed to be.

An oceanfront and very secluded property on Cannon Beach, our new house was too fucking big. It had five bedrooms, four bathrooms, and a kitchen that felt like the entire town of Cold could fit inside.

Don't get me wrong, it also had big, floor-to-ceiling windows that provided breathtaking views of the water, but it had more space than we really needed.

More space than anyone probably needed, to be honest.

But once Ivy had laid her eyes on the giant clawfoot tub inside the private master bathroom with panoramic views of the ocean, there was no other option.

She wanted it, and I wanted to give her everything she wanted.

I never would have thought a bathtub would be the catalyst for a big-ass real estate purchase, but I also never would have thought a lot of fucking things that had happened in my life would have actually happened.

I'd given up on predicting the future and found peace in enjoying every minute of the present with the most beautiful, stubborn, feisty woman I'd ever laid eyes on.

Lately, I'd just been striving to go with the flow and savor all of the good memories Ivy and I were creating together.

Some days were harder than others.

Some days, the painful shit of my past would try to hover over me like a thunderstorm. And some days, I'd see Ivy struggling with grief and sadness over the loss of her sister.

But the bad days were coming fewer and farther between, and the good days, the beautiful moments we shared, eclipsed all the rest.

I glanced at the clock and saw it was nearing dinnertime.

We'd been unpacking boxes and settling into our new home for the past two days, and since Ivy had woken up this morning, she'd looked exhausted.

But, damn, my woman was determined and stubborn to her core.

For the past several hours, I'd attempted to get her to sit down and rest, but she kept mentioning shit about nesting. Pregnancy hormones were ruling her life at this point, and apparently, she wouldn't rest until the house was perfect for the babies' arrival.

We still had time. That was a fact.

She was six months pregnant with two little bambinos inside her ever-growing belly. Ivy's normally petite ankles were swelling by the minute, and I prayed we still had a good three months before our children made their big debut into the world.

But reasoning had no place in a multiples pregnancy.

Stubborn or not, Ivy needed to rest, preferably surrounded by warm water and bubbles inside that clawfoot tub she loved so much.

"Baby!" I called over my shoulder from the master bedroom. "Where are you?"

No answer.

Last I'd seen her, Ivy had been organizing cutlery and Tupperware in the kitchen.

This shelf can wait, I thought and set down my hammer and nails before striding out of the bedroom in search of my pregnant wife.

Well, she wasn't actually my wife, but it wasn't for my lack of asking.

I'd proposed to Ivy more times than I could count over the past month, and every time she'd told me no.

She was hell-bent on waiting until after the babies were born.

Some shit about not wanting to be fat on our wedding day.

But she wasn't fat. She was pregnant. Beautifully pregnant with my two kids inside her. Honestly, in my eyes, Ivy had never looked more beautiful or sexy as she did right fucking now, belly swollen and skin glowing with our babies. But, as I'd been informed, I had absolutely no say when it came to the importance of wedding fashion.

Once I reached the downstairs, I passed the dining room and the kitchen, and still, no sign of Ivy.

"Baby!" I called again, and this time, I actually got a response.

"Out here! On the deck!"

Walking into the living room, I found two of the French doors opened up and letting in the late afternoon rays of the sun and the fresh breeze from the water.

And there, out on the deck overlooking the sea, stood Ivy, moving around white Adirondack chairs like a complete lunatic who seemed to have forgotten she was six months pregnant.

Her hair was red again, the blond dye making its exit after growing out three or four inches. While it had grown, so had Ivy's emotional stability. The change had been needed then, but the more she thought about it, the more she realized looking like Camilla wasn't a bad thing. Now, the long fiery locks lay down past her shoulders, shimmering beneath the sun.

Memories of the feisty woman who had sped into Cold, Montana with a lead foot leading her way filled my head, and I smiled.

It all felt like so long ago, and it was poignant reminder of not only all that we'd been through, but how far we'd come too.

"What are you doing?" I questioned as I stepped outside. "Stop moving that shit around, Ivy. You're too pregnant to be doing that."

She rolled her eyes. "The chairs aren't that heavy, and I won't know where I want them until I test out a few spots."

"Baby, they're just deck chairs. They can go any-fucking-where."

She glanced over her shoulder and narrowed her eyes. "They can't just go *any-fucking-where*, Levi. They need to be perfect before the babies get here."

I wanted to laugh at the absurdity. "I don't think the babies will get much use out of those chairs."

Her narrowed eyes turned to a full-on glare as she stopped fiddling with those goddamn chairs and turned on her heels to face me.

Glare be damned, I couldn't stop myself from drinking in the sight of her.

Her gorgeous and still-growing tits nearly spilling out of her tank top, bare legs, and swollen belly protruding over her unbuttoned jean shorts, she looked so beautiful it made my chest ache.

"Levi," she said, but I could barely hear her. I was too busy soaking up every little detail of her beauty. "I know it's crazy, but I need everything to be perfect."

"Everything is perfect," I said and stepped toward her. "Especially you. You're so fucking perfect."

She rolled her eyes and clucked her tongue. "Stop trying to be all sweet right now."

"I can't help it." I placed my hands on her tiny hips and stared down at the round ball of her belly that separated us for a few loving moments. I smiled and lifted my gaze to hers. "You're so beautiful, Ivy."

"You're just saying that," she retorted, and I shook my head without hesitation.

"You know me better than that," I said and pressed a soft kiss to her unsuspecting lips. "I don't just say anything, and when I do say something, I mean it."

The round apples of her cheeks blushed pink, and my heart flipped and turned beneath my ribs.

"How about we take a little break?" I suggested and moved my hands to the tight skin of her belly, gently rubbing tiny circles with my thumbs. "I'll run a bath for you and order some takeout, and we can spend the rest of the night just enjoying being in our new home."

"Can we eat on the deck?"

"We can eat wherever you want." I nodded and kissed her lips.

"Can we order Mexican?"

"Anything you want, baby."

"You're very good at being accommodating," she teased. I just grinned.

"Considering you're carrying around not one but two of my kids, I think you deserve all of the accommodation I can manage."

She quirked a brow. "And how much can you manage?"

"What exactly do you have in mind?"

"A foot massage."

"While you're in the bath or after?"

"I get to choose?" she exclaimed. "Holy moly, I love accommodating Levi! I should stay pregnant forever!"

I smirked, but then, lips to hers, I slid my tongue across the seam of her mouth until she let me push past her lips and take a taste. She moaned and wrapped her arms around my neck, and when I pulled away, those full, pink lips of hers were pressed out into a little pout.

"You're an asshole."

"What?" I questioned. "Why?"

"Because you get me all horny and shit, and then you stop!" She shoved at my chest, but I grabbed her wrist and held it gently.

"You know you can ask for something else besides a foot massage…"

"What do you mean?" She scrunched up her little nose. "Like a back massage?"

"Nuh-uh." I shook my head. "A *clit* massage."

Her eyes went wide, and those cheeks of hers flushed pink again.

"My mouth. Your pussy," I whispered. "Doesn't that sound nice?"

"Yeah. Okay," she said and nearly dragged me back toward the house. "Move it or lose it, buddy. We need to get upstairs, and we need to do it right fucking now!"

I grinned.

Besides the need to make everything perfect, there was one other constant with pregnant Ivy.

Sex.

She loved it. Needed it. Wanted it all day, every day.

And hell if I didn't love every goddamn second of it.

By the time we reached the bedroom, she was already shucking out of her tank top, jean shorts, and panties, and kicking her flip-flops off her feet and across the room.

I grinned, and I followed her lead and removed all of my clothes.

She stood before me, and my cock grew rock hard at the sight.

Soft, bare skin and round, pregnant belly. Full, heavy tits and erect, rosebud nipples. She was a fucking goddess.

I pitied every man in the world because they'd never get to experience the sight of Ivy naked, aroused, and with so much fucking heat in her eyes, I thought she might hold the power to burst my skin into flames.

"Beautiful," I whispered. "So goddamn beautiful."

She blushed at my words, and I licked my lips as I moved toward her.

"Turn around, baby," I demanded. "Hands on the bed to steady yourself and put that gorgeous fucking ass of yours in the air."

She did as I asked, and I just about growled when I saw her splayed out like that for me.

With my hands on her hips and my hard cock pressed against her ass, I leaned forward and started placing hot kisses down her back, her ass, and when I moved down between her legs, I leaned forward and pressed my face to her little cunt.

She was wet. So fucking wet.

And I had to take a taste.

With one long lick of my tongue, I groaned when her sweetness assaulted my senses. "God, you taste so good."

I took another taste.

And then another.

And then another.

She moaned and whimpered, and her hips started moving of their own accord.

Her pussy glistened and beckoned for my mouth, but I knew my baby was too worked up to take things slow.

She needed it fast.

She needed it hard.

And she needed it right fucking now. Trust me, I was more than happy to oblige.

Back to my feet, I grasped her small hips and slowly eased myself inside of her.

She let out a guttural moan, and her pussy milked the head of my cock. It felt so damn good I had to shut my eyes briefly and grit my teeth to regain my focus.

"This what you want?" I asked, thrusting forward a little, and she responded by pushing her ass back toward me, urging my cock to go deeper. I grinned. "You need it, baby?"

She mewled, and I responded by pushing myself to the hilt in one hard but smooth drive forward. "Oh God, yes, Levi," she said through another moan. "Keep going. Please, for the love of God, don't stop. Never stop."

I reached forward and let her full, heavy tits fill my big hands, and I couldn't stop the accompanying growl that left my lungs when I felt her lush fucking curves against my palms.

"More," she begged, and I was damn near drunk off my need for her.

I drove forward again and again and again.

And when her moans grew louder and raspier and delirious with pleasure, I lost it.

I couldn't hold back.

I let myself chase pleasure, both hers and mine, and I didn't stop until her pussy clenched tight around me, rippling against my shaft with her climax, and I was emptying myself deep inside of her on a guttural groan.

Heaven. Pure fucking heaven.

CHAPTER
TWENTY

Ivy

WITH MY PREGNANT BELLY GUIDING ME, I STEPPED INTO THE clawfoot tub in our master en suite. Bubbles and warm water and the kind of master bathroom Pinterest dreams were made of, this scene was pretty damn close to what I imagined heaven looked like.

This tub, let me tell you, was a dream.

And if I was being honest, it was probably the main reason we'd purchased this home.

I didn't know if it had been the pregnancy hormones talking or the fact that I'd known this gorgeous, extra wide porcelain bathtub would become one of my favorite places for peace and serenity.

But I guessed it didn't really matter.

We had the house.

And I had my heavenly clawfoot tub.

In all actuality, it was a great house in an amazing little beachside town. Between the award-winning schools and the gorgeous landscape of sea and mountains and lush nature and the small-town, laid-back vibe, it was a great place to raise a family.

The perfect place for Levi and me and our children.

Plus, I imagined once our two babies entered the world, I'd need a hot bath every now and then to keep my sanity. My mother, along with pretty much anyone else who knew I was pregnant, had already warned me just one little newborn was a lot of work, but Levi and I were apparently overachievers and had decided to go all out and create two tiny people at the same freaking time.

Once my body was fully submerged in deliciously warm water and vanilla-scented bubbles, and only the very top of my rounded belly peeked out above the water, I sighed. It was a wistful, sated sigh, and Levi didn't miss it.

"That good?" he questioned, sliding a white ottoman over to the edge of the tub and sitting down near my feet.

It was *all* good. The ah-mazing sex we'd just had twenty minutes ago. This perfect bath. Every-fucking-thing.

"I'm glad we bought this house."

He chuckled. "That damn bathtub was why we bought this house."

"It's not the *only* reason." I rolled my eyes and slid my hand through the bubbles, watching in awe as they clung to the tips of my fingers.

His blue eyes danced with amusement. "The instant you walked into this bathroom and spotted this damn tub, you literally said, *We'll take it!*"

He had a point. But that didn't mean I needed to let him know he was right.

"I don't remember that."

"Uh-huh," he said and smirked like the sexiest devil I'd ever seen. "Sure, you don't, you little liar."

"Even if this was the reason, which I'm not saying it is, there are other amazing things about this house. You can't deny that."

"Baby," he said, and his midnight-blue eyes locked with mine. "You know why I love this house?"

"Why?"

"Because you're in this house," he said. "The rest is just minor details."

"God, that's…that's so sweet, Levi." My heart pounded inside my chest and found its way into my eyes. "And alarming that you think everything else is just details. We have *twins* on the way."

He laughed. "It's the truth. You're my whole world." He rubbed his hand across my rounded belly. "You and these two little babies that, trust me, I haven't forgotten about."

I placed my hand over his. "I love you."

"I know," he said with a sexy, confident smirk, but before I could offer a sarcastic, irrational retort about being unloved, he added, "And I love you too. So you can go ahead and swipe that cute little pout off your lips."

Was I really pouting?

I traced my bottom lip with my wet fingertips and found my answer.

A full-on, puppy-dog pout.

Man, I was kind of ridiculous.

I blamed the hormones.

His playful blue gaze met mine, and I narrowed my eyes. "You know you shouldn't test my patience when I'm all hopped up on pregnancy hormones and bigger than a house."

"You're crazy, baby." With a soft chuckle and slight shake of his head, he reached into the tub, and with a washcloth lathered in my favorite body wash, started gently washing my propped-up feet.

"Levi Fox, you know, *you fucking know,* you should never call a pregnant woman crazy. That is just a recipe for an all-out war."

He grinned. "You're my favorite kind of crazy. That better?"

"Not really."

He rolled his eyes. "I love your crazy, baby. And I love your body. I've never seen you more fucking beautiful than you are right now."

I puffed out an annoyed breath. "My ankles are swollen. My

stomach is huge. And my face is getting fatter by the day. So, I call bullshit on your sweet, but very big fucking lies."

I was nearing my third trimester. My belly felt enormous—*because, hello, two freaking babies are growing inside of me.* My boobs were bigger than my head.

And, honestly, I had no clue what my ass looked like. But one could only assume, if it was growing like the front half of my body, it had gained more than a few inches on its already generous curves.

I was pregnant.

So. Fucking. Pregnant.

He locked his gaze with mine. "Just deal with it, baby. You're the most beautiful woman in the whole goddamn world to me."

"Pffft. That's because you're biased."

"Now, that *is* the truth. But is me being biased a bad thing?" he questioned, and he massaged the cotton cloth across my feet.

I shrugged. "I guess not."

"No, baby, it's definitely not," he said through a soft chuckle. "It means I'm hopelessly, undeniably, without a fucking doubt, in love with you."

This man, sometimes he could say the sweetest, most thoughtful fucking things.

And I couldn't not smile at his words.

"Love me forever?" I asked and he smiled.

"Always."

The cotton cloth brushed across the arch of my right foot, and I giggled from the ticklish sensations that ran across my skin.

Levi smirked and looked up at me from beneath his lashes. "Ticklish?"

"Just a little."

"I'm glad you finally agreed to sit your little ass down and rest. You needed it," he said and started to move the washcloth up to my calves, alternating both legs with a gentle massage and soft scrub. "And I know you don't want to hear this, but over the next few months, until our babies are born, you're going to have to start taking it easy."

"I know." I sighed. "It's just so hard. There are so many things I want to make sure get done before they get here and…" I paused and rubbed both hands across my belly. "I just want everything to be perfect."

Over the past few weeks, I had really started to notice the physical restrictions of carrying twins. And even though I kind of hated to admit it, Levi was right. I couldn't keep going full throttle. I couldn't stay on my feet for hours on end without much of a break. I had to cut it back a little.

"It will be," he said. "But how about you focus more on making the list of things you want done, and let me handle the actual work part of it, okay?"

"Okay."

I knew, more than anyone probably, that Levi Fox had a cold side to him.

He could be a Grade A asshole.

But once you peeled past his layers of undeserving guilt and pain and avoidance, he was just a beautiful man with a big fucking heart.

When he loved someone, he loved them fiercely. And it was moments like these, sitting in the bath watching Levi take care of me, that I realized just how far we'd come.

From fighting to kissing to fighting and kissing.

From heartbreak and turmoil to love and adoration.

From absolute devastation to tiny miracles.

Somehow, someway, we'd managed to get *here*.

I never used to believe in destiny or fate, but the way Levi's and my stars had miraculously aligned, it was hard *not* to believe there was some other, supernatural force pulling us together.

While Levi washed my legs, I leaned my head back on the edge of the tub and just let my muscles relax. God, it felt so good. The way his hands moved up and down my legs, massaging all of the spots that ached and throbbed from our busy day of unpacking.

I hadn't realized how much I'd needed this bath until right now.

And right on cue, both babies started to move inside my belly.

Bedtime, naptime, basically, any time I was trying to rest or relax, that was when our little chickadees decided to throw a party.

Kicks to the ribs.

Jabs to my bladder.

Two active babies and my uterus might as well have been a UFC arena.

You named it, I felt it. And sometimes, I felt it so hard I literally peed myself.

"Oh!" I yelped when I felt one especially powerful punch to my side.

Luckily, this wasn't one of those accidental piss scenarios.

Just pain. Sharp, stabbing, shooting pain.

Levi looked up, confusion and worry in his eyes, but I nodded down toward my now visibly moving belly.

"The babies are moving like crazy," I said. "It's a good thing I already love them so much."

He chuckled softly and stared down at my belly. His blue eyes turned mesmerized by the rolling motions and little jabs appearing beneath my skin.

"God, that's amazing," he whispered and reached out to rest both hands on my belly. "I can't believe there're two little lives inside there. Two tiny people that we made."

"I'm literally the miracle of life right now," I teased, but as I watched him closely, loving on and smiling down at my belly, I couldn't not smile.

"I can't wait to meet them."

"Me either." My smile turned full-on face grin—eyes, cheeks, hell, even my ears probably joined in on the happy expression.

"God, I'm one lucky bastard."

"This is true," I teased again, but his eyes turned serious. And instantly, I knew what the next words out of his mouth were going to be.

"Marry me, Ivy," he whispered and placed soft kisses on my belly. "Pretty sure I already know your answer, but I'm still asking. So, Ivy Stone, will you marry me?"

He'd been asking me nearly every day for the past few weeks or so, and every time, I said no. Not because I didn't want to marry Levi.

I did. I couldn't see my future without him in it.

I just didn't want to get married right now, while I was waddling like a penguin and as big as a whale.

Also, I didn't want him to ask me out of obligation. Which was completely stupid, I knew, but I couldn't help. Pregnancy made me a little bit irrational in my thought process. Way more fucking emotional than was my norm, that was for damn sure.

"No," I whispered back, and he just grinned. "I will marry you. Someday soon. Someday real soon. But not right now, not when I'm pregnant."

"So...no?"

"Nope." I shook my head and slid farther into the water, letting it block out the sounds around me.

Levi stared down at me, smiling like a loon. "You're mean," he said, but it was mostly muffled.

I just giggled, and eventually, I slid my head back out of the water so I could actually hear him.

"You won't even accept an engagement ring?"

"Nope."

"God, you're stubborn," he said, still grinning.

"We don't need an engagement," I explained. "Once the babies are born, I give you full freedom to whisk me away somewhere private, just the two of us, so we can get married."

"Promise?"

"Promise."

"I'm holding you to this, my soon-to-be wife."

I winked. "I hope you do, my soon-to-be husband."

Levi leaned forward and pressed a soft kiss to my lips, and I pretty much melted.

God, whenever he kissed me, it was like my brain lit on fire and the warmth spread like wildfire throughout my entire body.

I would spend the rest of my life kissing this man, of that I was certain.

CHAPTER
TWENTY-ONE

Levi

October 3rd, 2016

W HILE IVY HAD CONDUCTED NUMEROUS PHONE CALLS WITH her agent and publicist and a bunch of other Hollywood types I didn't understand, I'd been painting the nursery. She'd chosen the paint color, and to be honest, to me, it just looked like we were repainting the walls white. But if you asked Ivy, she'd adamantly disagree and tell you it wasn't white; it was the perfect shade of cream. *Warm, cozy, baby nursery cream.*

I couldn't tell the difference, but I knew when to pick my battles with a pregnant Ivy.

And questioning the color of the nursery wasn't worth the risk to my balls.

So, I'd painted all morning and kept my mouth shut.

Once I cleaned off the brushes in the utility sink near the garage, I walked into the kitchen to find Ivy standing near the stove.

"Hungry?" she asked as I sat down on one of the barstools near the island.

"You making lunch?"

"Yep." She reached down to the lower cabinet to pull out a pan, and instantly, I knew what our lunch would most likely entail.

Some sort of variation of eggs. Since eggs were a food she'd been eating daily for years, I'd have thought she wouldn't be able to take her obsession with them much further. But I'd been wrong. Her pregnancy diet was like her regular diet on steroids, and we ate fucking eggs *all* the goddamn time.

Scrambled. Over easy. Fried. Hard boiled. In an omelet. Breakfast, lunch, and dinner.

She had a few other foods that made appearances from time to time—green pepper, string cheese, tortillas—but they were nothing more than secondary characters in a play about eggs.

None of it made sense, but I just rolled with it.

"What are you making?" I asked, even though I already knew the answer.

She walked over to the fridge and started pulling out items and setting them on the counter beside her. First, the carton of eggs. Then, a bag of shredded cheddar cheese and a green pepper. And the million-dollar prize goes to? Levi Fox.

"What did you say?" she questioned once she'd gathered everything she needed to make an omelet.

"Well..." I paused and grinned. "I started to ask what you're making, but I'm pretty sure I have that figured out now." I nodded down toward the items she'd rearranged near the stove on the kitchen island.

She looked down, and a smile crested her pretty cheeks. "Am I that transparent?"

"Just a little bit."

"Apparently, pregnancy makes me a creature of habit," she responded and switched on the stove.

"Yeah, but in your defense, eggs were already your thing before."

"Could you imagine if these babies didn't like eggs?" she questioned, and her eyes widened in shock. "What in the hell would I have done for nine months?"

"Eat chicken," I teased, and her lips turned down into a scowl.

"Ew." She grimaced. "For the love of God, don't even talk about chicken unless you want me to hurl across the kitchen."

I grinned, and she lifted her right hand to flip me off, before refocusing her gaze on the task at hand. Eggs.

With a crack of four shells, she filled a small white bowl with the egg whites and yolks. But after she added the milk and started to whisk it all together, I noticed that her free hand moved to her lower back. She rubbed and pressed against a spot I assumed was tender, and that was when I decided to hop up from my barstool and take over.

"Why don't you go sit down, and I'll finish this?" I questioned, but it wasn't really a question since I would not take no for an answer.

"I'm fine, Levi," she said, voice one hundred percent annoyed, but when her brow pinched together in discomfort, I placed my hand to her belly and looked down at her in concern.

"Are you okay?"

She nodded. "I'm fine. Promise. Just a little uncomfortable."

"What do you mean by a little uncomfortable?"

"Because I'm carrying around two freaking babies," she retorted, her tone all sass.

"Are you having contractions?"

"No," she refuted, but I wasn't all that convinced.

But what in the hell did I know? I wasn't an expert in pregnancies. Especially, a multiples pregnancy.

"Go sit down, and I'll finish lunch."

"But—"

"That wasn't a question, baby."

The free hand to her back moved to her hip. "Are you bossing me around?"

"Only because I'm worried about you."

She groaned and handed me the whisk. "God, you're such a

caveman sometimes."

I kissed the top of her nose and grinned. "For you, yes."

But she didn't even make it to the kitchen table before she paused and gripped her belly.

"Ivy?"

She waved me off with a hand. "I'm fine," she said, but her face said otherwise. Her lips were pursed, and her face was tight with discomfort.

"You don't look fine," I said and set down the whisk to walk over toward her. With gentle hands, I guided her toward the chair and urged her to sit down.

Ivy sighed and leaned her back against the chair, but a few moments later, she hunched over slightly, and her face turned pained.

"Baby, I don't think this is normal."

She shook her head. "I don't think so either."

"You want me to call the doctor?"

She nodded. "Yes."

I didn't waste any time and snagged her phone off the counter. I scrolled through her list of contacts, and the instant I spotted Dr. Morrow, the obstetrician she'd found as soon as we'd moved to town thanks to a recommendation from Dr. Macintosh, I tapped the screen to call.

With the phone pressed to my ear, I looked over at Ivy and saw her situation hadn't gotten any better. She groaned and held her belly tightly again, her lips pursed as she breathed through the pain.

My heart dropped at the sight of it.

Fucking hell, the mere idea of something going wrong during Ivy's pregnancy had my chest growing tight with anxiety.

"Dr. Morrow," the doctor greeted on the third ring.

"Hey, Dr. Morrow. This is Levi Fox, and I'm calling because Ivy is having a lot of discomfort. It seems like she's having contractions."

"Are they painful enough that she has to breathe through them?"

"Yeah."

"And how long has she been having them?" she asked, and I looked at Ivy.

"How long have you been having contractions, Ivy?"

"I don't know." She shrugged and groaned again. "A few hours or so, I think. But they just recently got this painful."

Jesus Christ. A few hours? Even though I wanted to tell her she shouldn't have waited so damn long to tell me, I kept my mouth shut and focused on the task at hand.

"She said it's been a few hours," I told the doctor.

"And just remind me, is Ivy seven or eight months along?"

"She's just a little over seven months."

"I want you to go ahead and come to the hospital. I'm here now doing a delivery, and I can check Ivy out and make sure everything is okay."

"Okay. Thanks, Dr. Morrow. We'll see you soon."

■

After three hours of monitoring and two examinations by Dr. Morrow, we sat inside one of the triage rooms in the maternity ward waiting for the doctor to come back in and talk to us.

Ivy lay in the hospital bed, her body finally relaxed and her contractions slowed to a complete stop.

The doctor stepped inside, Ivy's chart in her hands.

"How are you feeling, Ivy?" she asked.

"A lot better."

Dr. Morrow stepped over to the contraction and fetal heart monitor and scanned the pages upon pages of recordings.

"Well, it looks like the medicine stopped your contractions, and both babies are doing just fine," she updated. "When you got here, you weren't dilated at all, but on my last check, you were a little over one centimeter. So, it's very apparent you were definitely having preterm labor. Luckily, we were able to stop it."

"Preterm labor?" I asked, and Dr. Morrow nodded.

"Yes," she answered and set Ivy's chart down on the table to give me her full attention. "This is very common in a twins pregnancy, and to be honest, I expected this to happen."

"So what do we do now?" Ivy asked.

"Well, now, you have to stay on bed rest until you deliver."

"Bed rest?" Ivy asked, and her lips turned down in a little frown.

"Yes, you're going to have to stay off your feet as much as possible and let this guy right here do most things for you," the doctor said and smiled over at me. "But the good news is that you don't have to stay here to do that. You can still be in the comfort of your own home."

Ivy sighed. "Well, I guess that's better than nothing, huh?"

"Yeah." Dr. Morrow smiled. "It's better than having to live in the hospital for the next few months. Trust me, I have to sleep here when I'm on call, and it's no beach resort vacation."

Both Ivy and Dr. Morrow laughed.

But I couldn't find the energy to join in.

As I sat there, listening to Ivy talk to Dr. Morrow about her bed rest restrictions, I couldn't stop my mind from drifting to worrisome territories.

It was like, all at once, it hit me.

Sitting right there, on that hospital bed, was my entire life.

Ivy. My babies. My whole fucking world.

I offered up a silent prayer.

God, please let everything go okay. Please keep Ivy and the babies safe. Please let the rest of this pregnancy go smoothly.

CHAPTER
TWENTY-TWO

Ivy

October 28th, 2016

WHILE LEVI FINISHED BUILDING THE SECOND CRIB, I SAT IN THE cozy, cushioned cream rocking chair with my feet—more like swollen sausages—resting on the matching ottoman.

He'd been hard at work all day, and all I could do was sit back and watch.

I hated it.

"This would be a lot easier if I could actually help get the nursery ready."

Levi glanced over his shoulder and grinned. "Bed rest, baby. Doctor's orders."

"God." I sighed, a deep cavernous breath out of my lungs. "I'm so fucking tired of being on bed rest."

"It's not too much longer," he said, and I wanted to smack him.

It was irrational, sure. But I was a hormonal as hell woman who was eight months pregnant with twins. Surely, that gave me grounds to be insane and unreasonable sometimes.

Unfortunately, he was on the opposite end of the room, and per doctor's orders, I was supposed to keep my ass seated and my feet up.

Not too much longer? Per Dr. Morrow, if I was a good patient and kept myself on bed rest and the babies continued to grow and develop like they should, I might be able to reach the thirty-eight-week mark before I delivered.

That was nearly a month away.

You'd think bed rest would be this glorious thing where you just got to sit around and be lazy and let everyone else wait on you hand and foot, but the glitz and glam of the slothful situation lost its shine about seven days in.

It was at that point that I quickly realized I had been served a house-arrest—wait, no a bed-arrest sentence.

A girl could only watch so many episodes of *The Office*, play so many games of Words with Friends, and surf the internet for so many hours in the day. Day after fucking day.

I was bored.

And slowly developing a chronic condition of cabin fever.

I wanted to go for a walk on the beach.

I wanted to go shopping for baby clothes.

I wanted to nest and help get the nursery ready.

I wanted to do every-fucking-thing but sit on my ever-growing ass and watch the world move around me.

Levi put the last screw into the crib and slid it over beside the other one.

All white wood and smooth edges, together, they looked amazing.

"What do you think?" he asked, and I smiled like a mother who couldn't wait to meet her babies.

"Perfect."

"And what about the armoire?" he questioned and nodded toward the wall by the door.

"Also perfect."

His smile was so full of pride it nearly made my heart burst.

God, this man, he was my rock.

While I'd been on bed rest and completely unable to help with anything, he'd been working his ass off to get our house, especially the nursery, together before the babies were born.

I'd tried to hire people, but Levi had outright refused. "This is my house, dammit," he'd said. "And I'll be damned if I'm going to pay some assholes to come in here and do work I'm more than capable of doing."

Obviously, I hadn't planned on hiring assholes, just, you know, *regular* guys, but it didn't matter.

Levi was a determined, stubborn, persistent, prideful kind of man, and when he set his mind to something, that was pretty much the end of it.

Over the past few weeks, I'd watched him paint nearly every room in our house. Refinish the hardwood floors in the living room. *And* build and assemble every piece of furniture in this room.

And that was just the shit I could remember off the top of my head.

"You did good, baby," I said and smiled at him from my lazy spot on the rocking chair.

"I did, didn't I?" he questioned and shot a cocky wink in my direction.

I just laughed, and he proceeded to move on to the next task, hanging the paintings I'd had Mariah purchase from a little boutique baby shop in LA. The instant I'd spotted these adorable little framed paintings of baby animals while browsing through Petit Tresor's online inventory, I had to have them.

Bunnies and lambs and fawns, they were so sweet and so freaking perfect for the soft, cream tones I'd picked out.

"You want all of these paintings on this wall?" Levi asked and I nodded.

The instant he hung up the first one, a picture of two baby

bunnies with their noses pressed together, I squealed from the cuteness.

"Oh my God, they are so perfect I might cry!"

Before I could stop myself, tears ran down my cheeks in a rush of happy, hormonal, pregnant as fuck emotions.

Good Lord, I can literally cry at anything these days.

"You okay over there?" he asked once his blue gaze met mine.

"Yeah…I'm just…so happy…" I sniffed and swiped at my tears.

He set down his hammer and nails and walked over to me with a soft smile etched across his full lips. Kneeling down beside me, Levi reached up and brushed a few rogue tears away from my cheeks. "You're so beautiful, Ivy."

A raspy laugh jumped straight out of my lungs. "I'm a mess," I said through the thick emotion sitting inside my throat. "I cry at everything. Even baby bunny pictures. It's pathetic."

He grinned. "You're pregnant. Beautiful as fuck and pregnant."

"More like pregnant as fuck."

"That too."

"It's all your fault," I said, and he raised his brow.

"All my fault?"

"Yep," I said and patted the top of my rounded belly with both hands. "You are the one who knocked me up."

He reached up and placed his hand over both of mine. "I'm so fucking glad I did."

I snorted and playfully shoved at his shoulder. "Yeah, that's easy for you to say. You're not the one who has to grow two humans inside of you."

Levi smirked and pressed a soft kiss to my lips. "You're doing such a good job, baby," he whispered against my lips. "I know it's hard. I know you're tired and frustrated and ready to not be on bed rest anymore, but just know, these babies are so lucky. They literally have the best mom in the entire world."

"You really think that?"

"I know that."

"Are you scared?" I asked. "Like, are you getting nervous about anything?"

He shook his head. "I'm not scared, just worried," he said and kissed the top of my nose. "I just want everything to go okay. I want you to be okay. I want the babies to be okay. I guess, if I'm scared about anything, it's the delivery."

"I'm a little scared too," I whispered. "About the delivery. About being a good mom. About having two newborns at the same time."

"You're the strongest woman I know with the biggest fucking heart. You've got this, Ivy," he said. "That, I'm certain of."

He rubbed his hand across my belly, and then leaned down to place his ear against the rounded edge of my stomach. His eyes stared up at me and shone with so much adoration it urged that familiar thickness into my throat.

"How are our babies today?" he asked and I shrugged.

"Just doing their normal hiccup song and jumping on my bladder dance."

"So, good?"

I nodded. "Definitely good."

"We need to name them," he whispered.

"I know."

"But it's pretty hard to name them when you refuse to let us find out what we're having."

"Oh God, not this again." I sighed and laughed and shoved at his shoulder. He lifted his head off my belly and just smirked down at me, before hopping to his feet and going back to the other side of the room to finish hanging the paintings.

"Well, you know I'm not wrong here," he said over his shoulder. "It'd be easier to figure out names if we knew what we're having."

"We just need to have some boys' and girls' names ready. And then, once they're born, I think we'll instantly know what to name them."

We'd been discussing baby names over the past few months.

It was a constant back-and-forth.

I'd love a name, but Levi hated it.

He'd think he'd found the perfect name, and I'd shoot him down because it was the same name of someone I knew—and didn't like—in high school or an ex-boyfriend or some other random reason that generally made him want to pull his hair out.

"Wyatt and Jack?"

"Nope."

"Hannah and Annie?"

Camilla had picked out the names of her kids when she was six years old, but they'd always been under lock and key like a state secret. Every time I tried to think of a name, I got a little sad I'd never managed to weasel the secret out of her.

But I guess that had been the whole point. She hadn't wanted me stealing them anyway.

"No."

"Ben and James?"

"It makes me think of Ben and Jerry."

"The ice cream?"

"Yep. And now, after you finish up in here, we need to go get some ice cream."

"You mean, I need to go get some ice cream."

"I'd go with you, baby, but doctor's orders, remember?" I teased him. "Plus, I'm not the one who brought up ice cream. You did."

"Pretty sure I never once said ice cream."

"That's not what I heard."

He laughed. "So, since you're already thinking about ice cream, I guess this means we're at a standstill with baby names?"

I shrugged. "It's all your fault, buddy."

Levi shook his head and held a nail to the wall. "Woman, I swear to God, you might be the death of me before this pregnancy is done."

"Oh, don't be so dramatic," I disagreed on a giggle. "You love me."

"That's true."

"And you want to get me ice cream."

Levi laughed. "Can you at least let me finish hanging these?"

"Uh-huh."

He smirked at me over his shoulder. "So kind of you."

That was me, the kindest woman in the whole wide world.

Well, maybe not. But Levi Fox made one thing clear—even with all the tragedy we'd faced, I was still one of the luckiest.

CHAPTER
TWENTY-THREE

Levi
November 28th, 2016

"OH MY GOD," IVY GROANED, AND I STARTLED AWAKE.

"Seriously?" she muttered to herself, bringing me further out from under the haze of peaceful dreams.

Quickly, I opened my eyes, and the soft glow of the early morning sun filtered in through the large windows of our bedroom.

"Everything okay, baby?" I asked and turned on my side to find her staring up at the ceiling, her brow pinched in frustration.

"No," she said and turned her irritated green gaze toward me. "Everything is not okay, Levi. I'm pretty sure I just sleep-peed."

"Sleep-peed?"

"Yes." She sighed a cavernous sigh and shut her eyes briefly. "Sleep-peed. As in, I just peed all over myself while I was sleeping."

It was moments like these that I realized just how much I loved Ivy.

She would always be the most beautiful woman I'd ever laid eyes on.

Even thirty-seven weeks pregnant with a belly so swollen it nearly tipped her over whenever she stood up.

And even when she was frustrated and bristling because she'd pissed all over our bed in the middle of the night.

Still, in my eyes, she was everything.

She searched my face, and her gaze turned to a glare. "Don't even think about laughing right now."

It took every inch of willpower inside my body not to smile or chuckle or show any signs of amusement on my end.

"I'm not," I said and sat up in bed. "And are you sure you peed, sweetheart?"

"I'm pretty sure. I mean, what else could it be?" she said, but it wasn't really a question. "Can you just help me out of bed so I can get out of these wet clothes and take a freaking shower?"

"Hold on," I said and decided to check the situation out myself. As I lifted the sheets, her eyes grew wide in shock, but I ignored it. My gut instinct told me this wasn't pee.

"W-what are you doing, you crazy bastard?" she questioned. "There's no need for you to see anything going on down there."

"Ivy," I coaxed. "Just let me check something real quick," I said as I moved down between her legs. Her pajama pants were soaked through, and I leaned forward to smell.

And just as I suspected, it definitely was not pee.

"Oh my God! Are you smelling my pee? That's so gross, Levi!"

"Pretty sure I've licked and kissed and fucked every inch of your body. So, smelling your piss is a non-issue for me." I grinned up at her. "And it's not piss, baby. I'm pretty sure your water broke."

Her eyes grew as wide as saucers. "What?" she questioned, downright shock consuming every inch of her face. But a few moments after, she moved both hands to her belly, and her mouth turned to a firm line.

"Are you having contractions?"

She shrugged, but when I placed both of my hands on her belly, I knew by the tightness of her abdominal muscles that she was.

"We need to call Dr. Morrow, Ivy," I said, and I couldn't stop my smile from consuming my face. "It looks like we're going to have our babies today."

"Our babies?" she asked, and her eyes turned shiny with emotion. "We're going to have our babies today?"

I nodded. "Yeah, sweetheart. I think today is the day we finally get to meet them."

She covered her mouth with her hand, and instantly, tears started to stream down her cheeks.

"What's wrong?" I asked and moved back up the bed to place both of my hands on her cheeks. "Why are you crying?"

"It just kind of hit me all at once." Her voice shook, and she swallowed against the thick emotions. "I'm going to be a mom. I'm going to have two tiny humans to take care of. Two little people who will need me and rely on me, and I just don't want to fuck anything up."

Her words hit me straight in the chest, and I smiled. "You won't fuck anything up, Ivy," I said, and she frowned.

"How do you know that?" she whispered. "What if I'm a bad mom?"

"That's impossible," I said and kissed her lips softly. "You are the strongest woman I've ever known, and I know without any doubts or uncertainties that you will be the very best mom to our babies."

"You think so?" she questioned, and her voice sounded so small it nearly made me cry.

"I know so, baby. Plus, you have nothing to be worried or scared about. You're not in this alone. I'm here, with you, every step of the way." I placed one last kiss to her lips before I moved off the bed. "Now, let's get you out of bed and into the shower, and I'll give Dr. Morrow a call to let her know what's going on."

"Oh my God," she whispered as I helped her to her feet. "I can't believe we're going to have our babies today."

"Best day ever."

"Yeah," she muttered and rolled her eyes. "That's easy for you to say. You don't have to push two humans out of your body."

I smirked down at her as I helped her into the bathroom. "There's my favorite feisty woman. I was wondering when she'd come back and give me hell."

Ivy laughed, and I turned on the shower.

But before I left the room to call the doctor, she grabbed my wrist and stopped me.

"I love you," she said.

"I love you too."

She slipped out of her soiled clothes and tossed them into the hamper. And just before she stepped underneath the warm spray of water, she said, "Now, go call the doctor and let her know I want one of those fucking epidurals as soon as I step foot into that hospital. I'm all for natural births and shit, but dear God, I refuse to try that route with two freaking human beings flying out of my body."

I grinned. "Duly noted."

Once I walked out of the bathroom, I dropped the tough guy act for a brief moment and let the shock consume me.

Holy shit. Ivy was going to have the babies today.

Our babies.

Before I called Dr. Morrow, I offered up a few words to the Big Guy upstairs.

"Please, God, let everything go okay," I prayed. "Please keep Ivy safe and our babies safe and just let this be an easy delivery for them. I wouldn't be able to survive if anything bad happened. So…*please*…I know I'm not the nicest person who has ever lived, and I've done some shitty things in my life, but please, just keep watch over them today."

Once I got that off my chest, I switched to the next top priority—getting Ivy to the hospital safely.

FOX

First, a call to Dr. Morrow.

Then, another quick one to Baylor. He'd made the move with us to Oregon to stay on as the head of our security team thanks to a small cash incentive, and I was incredibly thankful. Having someone we were familiar with—someone we trusted—protecting us was something wholly invaluable, and neither of us had had a problem with giving him the extra money.

And with the way the media and paparazzi had been waiting for news on Ivy's delivery, having Baylor at our backs was the most comforting thing I could think of.

■

Six hours later and Ivy was full speed ahead.

Once we'd arrived at the hospital, it'd been pretty obvious that Ivy's water had, in fact, broken. Her pants were wet again, and her contractions were getting stronger by the minute.

She'd been four centimeters dilated when Dr. Morrow had first checked her, and thanks to the swift and speedy care from the hospital staff, Ivy was inside of a delivery room and had an epidural.

She was thankful.

I was thankful.

And, I was certain by her colorful and very loud choice in words, everyone inside Cedar Hills Hospital was thankful.

Everything went lightning fast after that.

She'd been five centimeters by the time they had placed the epidural, and in what felt like no time at all, she was fully dilated and ready to start pushing.

Thankfully, the epidural was in full force, and the only thing she was feeling was pressure and the urge to push.

Now, we sat inside an OR room—because apparently, sometimes women had trouble delivering the second baby and needed a

C-section—and the soft, speedy heartbeats of our babies filled the room from the monitor.

It was a glorious fucking sound.

"Oh my God," Ivy moaned, and I reached out to grasp her hand that was currently gripping the side rail of her hospital bed, her white knuckles plainly visible. "I feel like a bowling ball is trying to shoot out of my vagina."

Dr. Morrow smiled down at her as she slipped on sterile gloves. "That's good, Ivy," she said. "Just breathe through all of that pressure while we get everything set up."

"I want to push so bad," she said through another moan.

"You're doing great, sweetie," Ivy's nurse Mindy said as she set up the stirrups. "Just keep breathing and making sure you're giving your babies all of that good oxygen."

A mere minute later, Ivy's legs were in stirrups, and Dr. Morrow was ready for delivery.

"Okay, Ivy," the doctor said. "Next contraction and you can start pushing."

"Oh, thank God."

I smiled down at her. "So proud of you, baby."

"Even though I yelled at the anesthesiologist and threatened to cut off his balls if he didn't get my epidural in?"

In her defense, it'd taken him three attempts, and her contractions had been coming every two to three minutes.

I chuckled. "Yep. Even after that." I kissed her forehead and whispered into her ear, "Strongest woman I know."

"Okay, yeah, I definitely need to push," she said, and Dr. Morrow nodded.

"You got this, Ivy."

She took a big, deep breath, shut her eyes tightly, and with all of her might, she pushed. The nurses counted beside her, and once they reached ten, they encouraged Ivy to take a quick breath and start pushing again.

After three rounds, the contraction was nearly over, and Ivy was panting from the exertion.

"You're a quick learner," Dr. Morrow said. "Usually, it takes women a few pushes to really figure it out, but you were already moving Baby A with the first go. If you keep pushing like that, I think we'll have a baby soon."

I kissed the top of Ivy's forehead and brushed the sweaty strands of hair off her cheek. "You're such a badass," I whispered into her ear, and she just laughed and rolled her eyes.

"Oh yeah, total badass *with an epidural.*"

I chuckled, and so did Dr. Morrow.

"No one's judging you here," Mindy said beside her. "And, honestly, with a twin delivery, Dr. Morrow probably wouldn't have let you attempt a natural delivery."

"Very true," the doctor agreed. "Okay, Ivy, looks like you're having another one, take a big, deep breath and let the pressure build until you can't tolerate it anymore, then push just like you did last time."

Ivy nodded and did as instructed. And a few seconds later, she leaned forward and pushed with all of her might.

It only took another ten or so minutes before the nurses started moving around the room, grabbing supplies and placing a baby blanket over Ivy's chest.

"Okay, Ivy," Dr. Morrow said. "Next push and Baby A will be here."

Ivy looked up at me and smiled. "Are you ready?"

"I've never been more ready," I said. "Especially since you wouldn't let us find out what we're having. I'm dying to know if there're two boys or two girls in there."

She smiled, and I'd never been more proud of her than I was in that moment.

"Here comes another contraction, Ivy," Dr. Morrow said. "Go ahead and push. But this time, do more of a slow and steady push so the baby eases out, okay?"

Ivy leaned forward and pushed just like the doctor had instructed, and between one breath and the next, the room went from being nearly silent to filled with the soft, screeching sounds of a newborn baby's cry.

"Baby A is here!" Dr. Morrow said, and with both hands, she lifted our now screaming baby up in the air so both Ivy and I could see. "And it's a girl!"

A girl.

A baby girl.

A pink, gooey, wiggly, screaming baby girl with bright red hair like Ivy's.

"Oh my God!" Ivy cried, and tears streamed down her cheeks. "She's so loud and so, so, so beautiful! And she's a little ginger!"

I smiled and chuckled, and tears I couldn't stop started seeping from my eyes.

Dr. Morrow placed our daughter on Ivy's chest, and my heart had never felt so full as it did in that moment, watching Ivy stare down at our baby with nothing but love in her eyes.

It was bliss. And love. And everything.

Ivy kissed our daughter's forehead, and her eyes met mine. "She's perfect," she whispered, and I nodded.

"Just like her momma."

We stared at each other for a long, heartfelt moment, and I leaned down to place a kiss on Ivy's forehead and then my daughter's.

But the moment stopped before it even really started.

"Baby B's heart rate isn't recovering too well, Dr. Morrow," Mindy said, and the doctor looked up at the monitor.

The normally quick and steady *bum-bum-bum* I'd been used to had dropped down to a slow and sluggish pace.

"Is everything okay?" Ivy questioned, and Dr. Morrow nodded.

"Everything will be okay, Ivy. Baby B's heart rate has gone down a little, but we're watching everything closely."

I looked over at the monitor, and I could tell the green squiggly lines did not look the way they had ten minutes ago.

"Go ahead and give Ivy some oxygen," Dr. Morrow instructed the nursing staff.

"Just take some slow and deep breaths, Ivy, and help Baby B get as much oxygen as possible." Mindy placed an oxygen mask over Ivy's face, and I waited with bated breath for our baby's heart rate to go back up.

But it didn't.

If anything, it only got slower.

The mood shifted, and the medical staff switched from laid-back to quick and fast-acting.

More staff came into the room, and I felt like my heart had fallen straight out of my chest and onto the floor.

"W-what's happening?" I asked.

"Baby B isn't recovering like we'd hoped," Dr. Morrow responded and stood up from her doctor's stool. "If the baby were a little farther down, I'd say we could wait it out a little longer, but I'm not liking what I'm seeing right now. I think the safest thing is a C-section."

The doctor slipped off her gloves and looked over at Mindy. "Tell them we need the OR staff in here right now. I'm going to go scrub in real quick."

"A C-section?" Ivy questioned, and tears filled her eyes. "Is my baby going to be okay?"

Dr. Morrow moved toward her and placed her hand on Ivy's belly. "Ivy, I promise you, you're in good hands. I know this all seems a little scary right now, but we need to move pretty quickly to make sure we get the baby out safely, okay?"

Ivy nodded, but her lip quivered and her chin vibrated from her emotion.

Our daughter was taken from Ivy's arms and placed in the infant warmer, where another nurse was there to check her out.

And our other baby's heartbeat had never sounded slower.

Its sluggish rhythm resonated in the room, and I held my breath between each soft, slow beat that sang out from the monitor.

I was no doctor, but I knew it was too slow. Too fucking slow.

"I'm scared, Levi," Ivy said, and I just gripped her hand tightly.

"It's going to be okay, baby. Everything is going to be okay."

I tried to reassure her despite the fact that I wasn't reassured at all.

I was terrified.

A scant thirty seconds later, I was escorted out of the OR room while they got Ivy ready for surgery. I didn't understand why, but they said it was protocol, and they needed to make sure everything stayed sterile.

Initially, I'd just started out with a hair net, but now, they'd had me put on a mask, white shoe covers, and some sort of yellow gown over my clothes.

I had no idea what was going on.

All I knew was that both Ivy and my babies were inside of that OR room and I had no control over what happened.

It felt like a lifetime in that fucking hallway.

All the while, staff moved in and out of Ivy's OR room at a hurried pace.

I wanted to ask them what in the fuck was going on.

I wanted to demand that I go inside to be with Ivy.

But I knew that was counterproductive.

The medical staff needed to focus, and they didn't need an emotional and scared father getting in their way.

I paced the hallway.

And I paced some more.

By the time I felt like I'd died a thousand deaths inside that fucking hallway, nurse Mindy opened the door.

I looked up at her, heart clenched tight in my throat, and prepared myself for the worst. "Everything okay?"

She nodded and smiled. "Everything is okay."

"Really?" I asked, and a new onslaught of tears filled my eyes. "Ivy and the babies are okay?"

Her smile grew wider. "Your little Baby B had the cord wrapped around her neck, but Dr. Morrow was able to get her out quickly. And once we gave her a little oxygen, she started crying just as loud as her sister. Congratulations, Dad. You have two beautiful, healthy baby girls."

I lifted my hand to my chest. "Thank God," I whispered out like a prayer, and it felt as if the weight of the world fell off my shoulders in an instant.

"You ready to see them?"

"Yes."

Once I stepped into the OR room, not one, but two newborn cries filled my ears, and I burst into tears of relief and joy.

And there they were, two pink, wiggly, screaming baby girls beneath an infant warmer, while nurses stood around them, checking them out.

Thank God.

I wanted to kiss their little fingers and toes.

I wanted to hold them in my arms.

But before I went to my babies, I needed to see their beautiful momma.

I needed to see Ivy.

"Can I see her?" I asked, and Mindy nodded.

"You can sit in that chair right by her. Just be careful around the sterile drape and equipment because Dr. Morrow is still finishing up the surgery."

Carefully, I moved toward Ivy and sat down in the chair beside her head.

With glossy eyes, I gripped her hand and smiled down at her.

"You did it, baby. Two beautiful girls," I whispered and she smiled.

"Two beautiful, *ginger* girls."

Through my tears, I laughed.

"I love you so much, Ivy," I whispered and kissed the side of her mouth. "Thank you for making my life."

CHAPTER
TWENTY-FOUR

Ivy

November 29th, 2016

L EVI STOOD AT THE CORNER OF MY POSTPARTUM ROOM, STARING down at our tiny newborn daughters sleeping peacefully in their bassinettes.

Life. Was. Good.

"How are my daughters?" I asked, and he looked over his shoulder with a smile.

"Perfect and beautiful and sleeping," he said. "I swear to God, Ivy, they are the most perfect babies I've ever seen in my life."

That urged a big, huge smile to kiss my lips.

Even though I was stuck in this god-awful hospital bed, inside of my postpartum room, I had never been happier.

It'd been a hell of a delivery. And I'd really thought we were going to lose our daughter, but thankfully, Dr. Morrow had been quick to act, and when it was all said and done, both the babies and I were doing just fine.

Now, if only I could get back the feeling in my legs and get out of this fucking bed, that would be icing on the cake.

"How are you feeling?" Levi asked, and even though I was still a little groggy and my body felt like it'd been through the wringer, the answer was instant and easy.

"Perfect."

He quirked a brow. "Really?"

"Really."

He grinned. "Strongest woman I know."

"Happiest woman you know too," I said and then added, "Also, the hungriest. I could really use a cheeseburger and fries right about now…or pizza…or cookies…or basically, anything would be perfect at the moment."

He chuckled at that. "The nurse said you could start with some ice chips."

I pouted.

"Them's the rules, baby. You just had major surgery. You have to ease yourself back into it."

"Fucking hell," I groaned. "Having babies is no joke."

"The way you have them?" he questioned with a little smirk. "Yeah, it definitely is no joke."

But then his blue eyes got serious, and he moved away from the two plastic baby bassinettes sitting in the corner of the room and sat down on the edge of my bed. "I was so scared, Ivy," he whispered and grasped my hand with his. "I was so scared I was going to lose you or one of our girls. I think I aged ten years waiting outside that OR room."

I lifted my hand and pressed it to his cheek. "I'm okay. The girls are okay. There's nothing to worry about now."

He nodded, and his blue eyes sparkled with unshed tears. "Thank fuck for that."

"We really know how to bring the dramatics, huh?" I questioned to bring some levity to the situation.

"Yeah." He squinted his eyes in amusement. "But I guess since my wife is a famous actress, I should expect some drama."

I quirked a brow at that. "Your wife?"

"Yeah." He nodded. "My wife."

"Maybe I'm a little slow on the uptake, but I don't remember the wedding. Did Dr. Morrow marry us while she was putting my organs back in their rightful places?"

"Minor details, baby." Levi smirked and leaned forward to press a soft kiss to my lips. "In my heart, you're my wife. You're my whole fucking world."

"Ditto, honey."

"I'm your wife too?" he asked, voice teasing, and I grinned.

"Nope, but I'm hoping you'll be my husband," I said, and I locked my gaze with his. "Let's get married, Levi. As soon as we can fit it in, let's do it."

"Already planned on it, baby," he said with a sexy little smirk.

"What do you mean, already planned on it?" I asked and reached out to pinch the skin of his arm. "Like, you already have plans in the works?"

He just shrugged, but his eyes were full-on mischievous. "Don't worry about it."

"Levi Fox, have you made wedding plans for us already?"

"I said, don't worry about it. Let me handle the details.," he said and stood up from his spot on the bed.

"Oh my God," I groaned, but I couldn't hide the delirious amusement in my voice. "You're lucky my legs are still numb or else…"

"Or else what?"

"Or else I'd be out of this bed and forcing the secrets out of you."

"That sounds dirty, baby." He waggled his brows. "Can I get a rain check on that for like six to eight weeks from now?"

"You're ridiculous." I rolled my eyes, but I couldn't fight my giggles.

He smirked at me, but the moment didn't last long because a soft newborn cry started to fill the room. Shortly after that, both girls were crying.

Levi walked over to their bassinettes, and without any hesitation, he picked up both girls in his big, strong arms and started swaying them gently back and forth.

They weren't having it, though.

Their little cries only grew louder and stronger, and Levi smiled toward me.

"I think they want their beautiful momma," he said softly, and immediately, I reached out both of my hands.

"Bring them here."

Gently, he placed them in my arms, and I stared down at their two little faces with more love that I could've ever imagined.

"God, they are so beautiful," I whispered. "I just can't believe how much I love two tiny little people."

"I know," he agreed, and I looked up to find him smiling down at us. "And it looks like they just wanted to be with you."

I looked back down at the girls, and slowly, their eyes started to flutter closed, their cries softening to silence.

They were such dolls. Even just out of the womb, they were true redheaded beauties.

God, it was so hard to fathom, so hard to wrap my mind around these two little humans Levi and I had created. Instantly, I was near bursting with love for them, and my eyes shone with emotion.

My sweet, beautiful daughters filled me with a sunshine I had never known existed.

"I don't think I've ever been happier than I am right now, Levi."

"Me either, baby," he said and sat on the bed beside me. "Me either."

We stayed like that for a long moment, both of us gazing down at our babies and soaking up every little thing about them.

It wasn't until Levi's phone rang from the bedside table that we both broke from our blissful trance.

He grabbed it from the table and checked the screen.

"Looks like Grandpa Sam wants to FaceTime," he said with a grin. "You feel up to it?"

I nodded.

Levi clicked the green phone icon, and within seconds, Sam's smiling face filled the screen.

"Are the babies here?" he asked, completely forgoing pleasantries. "Tell me the babies are here, and I finally get to know if my great-grandbabies are girls or boys."

Great-grandbabies. I couldn't not smile at his words.

Although there was no familial relation, it felt right.

Sam was an important part of both Levi's and my lives.

Levi tilted the screen toward the two babies currently sleeping in my arms. "Here they are," he said, and I watched Sam's face fill with emotion.

Relief. Joy. And love. So much love.

"Those are girls," he said, and his voice shook. "I know, without a doubt, those are girls. The most beautiful girls I've ever seen in my life."

I smiled. "Definitely girls."

"God, they are something," he said. "Congratulations to both of you. And thank you for bringing these two beauties into my life. I couldn't be happier right now."

"Thanks, Sam," Levi said, and I smiled. "That means a lot."

"So...do these little ladies have names?"

"Yes," Levi answered, and his gaze locked with mine. Instantly, emotion and love and joy clogged my throat.

Before I'd gone into labor, we still hadn't known what we were going to name our babies. We'd tried. God, we'd tried. But we hadn't really found anything we loved.

But once our daughters made their big entrance into this even bigger world, we *knew*.

In hindsight, I honestly couldn't believe we hadn't known all along.

"Well..." Sam urged. "Are you going to tell me?"

I smiled and couldn't stop a few bittersweet tears from slipping down my cheeks as I prepared to tell him. "Sam, we'd like to introduce to you our beautiful, perfect daughters, Camilla and Grace."

Sam's eyes went wide, and then soon, he also had a few tears of his own streaming down his cheeks. "God, I'm just... I couldn't think of better names for them," he said, and his voice shook with his words. "Camilla and Grace. Two perfect names for two perfect girls."

I couldn't have agreed more.

The world wasn't fair. It wasn't fair at all. But sometimes... sometimes, it paid you back.

Hello, Hollywood!
Ivy Stone Birth News!

November 30th, 2016

A huge, heartfelt congratulations are in order for Ivy Stone and Levi Fox!

Just two days ago, they welcomed their beautiful identical twin *girls* into the world!

The twenty-nine-year-old Hollywood actress delivered her twin daughters with longtime boyfriend Levi Fox on November 28th in the late evening at Cedar Hills Hospital in Oregon.

According to an inside source, the delivery did have some complications, but both momma and her babies are healthy and doing well.

Talk about great news!

Our secret insider also updated both girls weighed *over six pounds.*

That's a whopping twelve pounds of baby that Ivy was carrying around!

We bow down to you, Ms. Stone!

We're all dying to know the names of Ivy Stone's baby girls, and we can't wait to see if they look like their beautiful mother or handsome father.

Ivy Stone's publicist has declined to comment on the recent birth, but we'll be on #NewbornStox first official photo and name watch. Expect more updates to come on this exciting news!

CHAPTER
TWENTY-FIVE

Levi

December 15th, 2016

O NCE I CLEANED UP THE KITCHEN AFTER DINNER AND TOOK A quick shower, I walked into our bedroom to find Ivy sound asleep, the script she'd planned on reading through sitting in her lap.

Her back still rested against the headboard, but her eyes were closed, and her head was just kind of leaned forward.

It'd been two weeks since we'd come home from the hospital, and I knew between recovering from surgery and breastfeeding and mothering two newborns, Ivy was exhausted.

After we'd had dinner, she'd insisted on getting a little work done, and even had high hopes of taking a shower herself. But obviously, sleep had sounded the most irresistible call of all.

I slid the script off of her lap, careful to keep it opened up to the last page she'd been on, and placed it on the nightstand. Gently, I eased her down onto the bed and pulled the blankets over her body.

She didn't even startle. Her body lax and her breaths soft and deep.

Work could wait.

A shower could wait.

Sleep was a must.

Once I ensured she was all settled, I turned off the lights, grabbed the baby monitor, and walked back downstairs.

But I only made it halfway down the steps before Camilla's soft cries started to reverberate through the speaker.

The thought of it made me smile. The fact that I already knew my daughters so well, I could distinguish their cries from one another.

But newborn babies cried *a lot*.

Pretty much every two to four hours for the first few weeks or so.

Sometimes, if we were lucky, they'd go five hours, but those amazing moments were few and far between right now.

I turned on my heels and moved back up the stairs and into the girls' nursery.

Camilla's little legs and arms were tensed with irritation, and her cries were starting to grow louder by the second. She was pissed. About what, I wasn't sure. But the girl had a track record of having quite the little temper.

Grace, on the other hand, was more laid-back. She didn't demand as much attention and tended to have a little more patience when she needed to be changed or fed.

But little Cami... Yeah, not so much.

Besides her mother, she was the cutest little diva I'd ever met.

I lifted a now screaming Cami out of her crib and into my arms, swaying her back and forth gently. "What's going on, little lady?"

She responded with a shriek, but eventually, her cries softened, and only her bottom lip quivered to show her frustration.

Ivy had fed both girls before she'd laid them down, so I had a feeling it was more a diaper situation than anything else.

"Let's get your diaper changed and see if that turns this feisty mood around," I whispered to her and moved her to the changing table.

Once I laid her on her back, I set to work on changing her diaper.

I'd learned pretty quick that twins required fast hands.

You couldn't do anything slow, and you generally always had to do everything twice.

No doubt, once I managed to get Cami settled, Grace would wake up with her own demands.

And it didn't take long for my prediction to come true.

Cami's fresh diaper had been fastened no more than ten seconds before Grace decided to let me know she was also pissed.

Although, her fury wasn't quite as sassy.

I placed Camilla back in her crib and got to work on appeasing little Grace.

Once both girls were calm and quiet, I arranged both of them in my arms and sat down in the cushioned rocking chair Ivy loved so much.

It was her favorite chair.

Apparently, it was *a dream for breastfeeding.*

Her words, not mine. Obviously, since I was lacking the equipment to have any expertise.

"Everyone happy now?" I asked and looked down at both of them.

Cami wiggled her little body, kicking out her legs a few times, and Grace stared up at me with big, wide eyes.

"I'll be honest, you little ladies can really give a man a run for his money," I whispered. "It's a full-time job keeping you both happy, probably even harder than being a cop and catching criminals. But you know what? It's the best damn job I've ever had."

Sleepless nights.

Crying babies.

Constant, organized chaos.

I was the luckiest man on the planet.

"God, you girls look so much like your momma, it's crazy," I said, staring down at them in awe. "Thank God for that, huh?"

Camilla blew a few spit bubbles, and Grace's little pink lips crested wide into a yawn.

"One day, I hope you'll be a little more interested in the things I have to say, but I have a feeling when you're teenagers, you'll be too busy driving me nuts."

For the longest moment, I just took them in.

These two little people that had my heart in their tiny hands.

They'd only been on this earth for mere weeks, and still, I was certain they had me wrapped around their fingers.

Hell, they had the whole world wrapped around their fingers.

"Did you know there's a whole bunch of people that want to get pictures of you and put them in magazines?" I asked, and both girls just stared up at me. "One magazine offered us one million dollars just to get a picture of you? How crazy is that?"

Both girls stared up at me, eyes wide. They obviously thought it was as batshit crazy as I did.

"Goddamn vultures," I muttered. "Like your momma or I would ever use our beautiful daughters for money. Hell, like we even give a shit about money. And," I added, "how about we keep the whole curse-word thing between us? Your mom is already on my ass about it."

Once news had broken that Ivy had gone to the hospital, and an unknown source inside the hospital had revealed our daughters had been born, it had been nothing less than constant requests for interviews and pictures and everything in between.

Magazines wanted the first official photo of the twins.

Gossip sites had published what felt like hundreds of posts about what were mostly incorrect facts about Ivy's birth and the girls' names.

Hell, Ivy had shown me one website that had posted fake nursery pictures, acting like they had gotten an exclusive on how the twins' room had been decorated.

It was fucking insanity.

And I was thankful we'd found our little slice of serene and very private heaven in Oregon.

If we'd been in LA, or hell, even Cold, it would have been intolerable.

It also helped that I was a bit paranoid about Ivy and the girls' safety, so I had increased security since we'd arrived home from the hospital.

We'd had enough bad shit happen to us in the past that I refused to leave anything to chance.

I'd rather be overprotective than stupid.

And when it came to the three most important people in my life, I'd stop at nothing to ensure their safety.

A little squeal of a cry left Cami's lips, and I glanced down at her to find she was doing her normal, restless, "I'm tired, but I don't know what to do" thing.

All of that sass and sometimes, she just exhausted herself to the point of full-on irritation. It reminded me a lot of Ivy, and I smiled at the thought.

"I have so many things to tell you girls. I can't wait to tell you about Grace and about your aunt Camilla. I just...I can't wait to put the whole world at your little feet."

Grace's eyes fluttered closed, but Camilla stayed wide-eyed and a little bit cranky. I rocked back and forth in the chair, and that seemed to appease her enough to soften her small whines until they slowly disappeared into silence.

Her eyes weren't closed, but she was at least calm.

And Grace, well, she was already sleeping.

FOX

Laid-back and feisty.

Sassy and relaxed.

Our girls may have been identical twins, but they were their very own little people.

And, God, I loved them like I had never loved anything before.

CHAPTER
TWENTY-SIX

Ivy

A NXIETY STARTLED ME AWAKE, AND I OPENED MY EYES TO A DARK, quiet bedroom.

What time is it? I wondered.

I felt like I'd been asleep for hours, possibly days, but when I snagged my phone off the nightstand and checked the time, it was only a little after nine.

I had no idea how long I'd been out cold, but the last thing I remembered was putting the girls in their cribs and reading through a new script Jason had sent over.

Sitting up on the side of the bed, I rubbed at my eyes and turned on the lamp.

The script I'd been reading lay open on the nightstand, and Levi was nowhere in sight. He'd hopped in the shower right before I'd sat on our bed, and I'd even had high hopes of taking a shower myself, but apparently, exhaustion had consumed me.

I guessed that was the story for most new moms, though.

It'd been a blissful, chaotic, yet sometimes rough two weeks.

Being a mom was hard fucking work in general. But being a mom and breastfeeding two newborns around the clock, well, it was quite the challenge.

One that I was thankful for every single day, but one hell of a task no less.

Slowly but surely, we were finding our way, though.

Levi and I had decided early on we would do this whole parenting thing without any help. We didn't want to do what most of my Hollywood friends did when they had kids. We didn't want a nanny raising our girls. We wanted to be the ones to care for them as much as physically possible.

But we weren't completely crazy. The first seven days after we'd gotten home from the hospital, my mom had stayed with us and helped out.

Which, yeah, that had been a godsend.

The soft sound of Levi's voice filtered in from the hallway, and my eyes perked up in curiosity. I could tell he was talking, but I had no idea who he was talking to.

On tired legs, I moved off the bed and into the hallway.

And instantly, I knew he was in the girls' nursery.

I tiptoed toward the room, and when I reached the partially open door, I peeked inside to find him sitting in the rocker, both girls in his arms.

Camilla stared up at him, wide-eyed as he spoke, while Grace appeared content and asleep.

"You have your momma's eyes," he whispered down to our sassiest daughter. "Big, huge eyes that will for sure break some hearts when you're older."

He smiled down at her, and my heart damn near melted in my chest.

When I'd first found out I was pregnant, I knew Levi had had some terrifying thoughts go through his head. He wanted to be a good parent to our babies. He didn't want to be distant like his father or completely absent like his mother.

Because of his childhood, he had some serious demons to

work through.

But in the end, he'd more than proved that our girls had the very best daddy in the whole world.

He was so attentive and loving and made sure we wanted for nothing.

All three of us.

"Do you want to know a secret, Cami?" he whispered down to our daughter.

Big eyes and parted little lips, she just looked up at him in awe.

"I'm going to marry your momma," he said softly, and my breath whooshed straight out of my lungs at his words. "Soon, I'm going to marry her. She has no idea when or where, but I do. I already have it all planned out."

My heart pounded wildly in my chest, and I couldn't hide the smile from my lips if I wanted to.

"But that's our little secret, okay?" he whispered and then leaned down to kiss the top of her little forehead.

My chest grew tight from the sudden growth of my heart. As I secretly stood there, watching Levi with our girls, I was certain I'd never loved him more than right now.

He was my world, my everything, and every day, my love for him grew inside of me.

We'd started out like a fucking wildfire.

We'd hated each other. We'd done cruel things and said cruel things, but the one constant that had always remained was that we were drawn to one another.

It was like we were each other's missing halves.

And while we'd fought it in the beginning, in the end, we couldn't deny we were meant to be.

Life had thrown us so many obstacles. So many terrible things.

So many life-altering situations that still left scars on both of our hearts, but there was no denying that when it came to us together, we could survive anything.

I knew life wouldn't always be easy.

Every day, for the rest of my life, I'd have to live with the fact that I'd never be able to talk to my best friend. I'd never be able to see my sister Camilla smile or hear her laugh or call her when I needed a shoulder to lean on.

I missed her like crazy, and there were moments when the grief of her loss felt so strong I thought I'd choke on it.

She'd never get to meet my daughters.

She'd never get to hold the niece I named after her.

I'd never get to see her have babies of her own or meet the man who would steal her heart.

So many moments I would never get to experience with her.

But despite all of the pain and grief and sadness that came with losing my twin sister, I still woke up every day looking forward to my life.

And that was all thanks to those three people sitting inside of that nursery.

My family.

My life.

I was lucky.

So, so lucky.

"Hey," Levi said when he looked up from the girls and met my eyes. "How long have you been standing there?"

I shrugged. "Not that long."

He quirked a brow. "Not that long?"

I smiled. "Don't worry, honey. Your secrets are safe with Cami."

The future looked vast and beautiful, and I had a feeling Levi and I would be just fine. No—we'd be more than fine. We'd be happy.

EPILOGUE

Levi

"**M**OM," IVY SAID INTO THE PHONE PRESSED TO HER EAR. "Did you know about this?" she asked and looked at me from across the living room inside the beach house I'd rented out for us for the week.

"You guys are so evil!" she said.

I had no idea what her mom said on the other end of the line, but I had a feeling whatever it was, it let Ivy know I'd had this plan in place for months now. Not to mention, her parents had helped.

This was about to be the best day of my life.

Today, I would officially make Ivy Stone my wife.

And thanks to her parents for watching the girls with Baylor's and Hampton's presence to assure their safety, we'd have seven days to enjoy our honeymoon. Alone. Without any distractions. On the most private, secluded, gorgeous fucking island I could find.

And when I say secluded, I mean, besides two of our other security guys and a few staff members inside the rented home, we'd have to take a thirty-minute boat ride before we'd see another soul.

I'd kept everything top secret. Only a handful of people even knew we were here.

Which meant there was no risk for paparazzi or any other unwelcome visitors.

It was fucking perfect.

"Are the girls doing okay?" Ivy asked her mom as I moved our suitcases into the master suite.

The house was open and airy, and with the patio doors open, a soft breeze filled with the scents of salt water and sun flowed throughout.

"What about Cami?" Ivy's voice echoed down the hall. "She's been a little fussy since I stopped breastfeeding. I just hope she doesn't give you a hard time this week. I mean, seven days is a long time to be away from her momma."

I knew Ivy had some anxiety about leaving the girls, but I also knew she needed this getaway. She needed some time to herself. We needed some time to ourselves. We needed to recharge and relax and just enjoy one another.

And fuck, I needed to marry her more than I needed to goddamn breathe.

"I know, Mom. You're right. And I'm so thankful you're watching them so Levi and I could get away," Ivy said, and I smiled.

Her mom was a saint, and I was just as thankful as Ivy that she and Dave would be caring for the girls this week.

No doubt, they were in good hands.

Surely, I wouldn't have been able to get Ivy on the private plane I'd chartered to get here if she hadn't felt like her daughters would be okay.

When it came to our girls, Ivy was full-on momma bear.

But that was exactly why she was the best fucking mom in the world.

"Please, just call me if you need anything, okay?" Ivy said. "Oh, and thanks a lot for not telling me that Levi was stealing me away to get married, you little devious liar. I can't believe you kept that from me!"

I grinned and walked into the master bathroom to take a quick shower.

I knew her phone conversation would most likely last another twenty minutes, and I needed to wash the hours and hours' worth of travel off of me.

By the time I was out of the shower and had thrown on a pair of black boxer briefs, Ivy was off the phone and outside.

Surrounded by sunshine and palm trees and white sand and clear blue water that went on for days, Ivy stood out on the balcony of the home and just stared at the beauty that lay at her feet.

Eyes wide and lips parted, she was completely awestruck.

I smiled as I stepped behind her and wrapped my arms around her waist, pulling her back against my chest. This was the exact reaction I'd hoped for.

"I can't believe you did this," she whispered and leaned her head against my chest, her big green eyes staring up at me. "Like, I knew you were up to something, but I had no idea it was this."

"I wanted it to be perfect."

"It's way fucking more than perfect, Levi Fox. It's just... Yeah... it's everything."

"You gonna marry me, baby?" I asked, smirking down at her. "Because if you're going to say no, then that's really going to put a damper on this week's plans."

"I'm gonna marry you *so hard*. You have no idea."

"Well, thank fuck for that," I teased. "It only took like a year for you to finally say yes."

"Pretty sure I'm worth the wait," she retorted, all sass.

"All good things come to those who wait?" I teased and pinched her ass.

She giggled. "Something like that."

I pinched her ass again, but then I kissed her nose. "I would have waited ten lifetimes to marry you," I said, and I meant every fucking word.

"Love you," she said and turned on her heels. She wrapped her arms around my waist and leaned up on her tippy-toes to place a soft kiss to my lips. "Thank you for being the most amazing man I've ever known."

"Love you too, baby," I whispered against her lips. "Now, go inside and get dressed because we only have about an hour until a minister is going to meet us out on that beach so I can officially make you mine."

"An hour?" she squeaked out, and her eyes narrowed. "Are you serious?"

"One hundred percent," I said over my shoulder as I walked back inside the house. "With how long it took for you to finally say yes, I sure as shit wasn't leaving anything to chance. I'm marrying you today, Ivy. And that's a fucking fact."

"You're such a caveman sometimes!" she yelled back to me, but her voice was more playful than anything else.

"Oh, just you wait, soon-to-be Mrs. Fox. Tonight is our wedding night, and I'm about to go full-on caveman when I'm devouring and claiming what's mine."

Ivy

"*Goddamn,*" Levi said as he slowly slipped off the little white cotton dress I'd worn for our ceremony. "I'm the luckiest fucking man that's ever lived."

I smiled. And then, well, I shivered.

Because, holy hell, Levi Fox was *my husband.*

He was mine.

All fucking mine.

And now, this sexy, handsome man was slowly slipping off my white lace panties and staring down at me like a man starved to devour the buffet that was me.

"You're so beautiful, Ivy," he whispered. He stood behind me now, and his lips trailed a delicious path of hot kisses down my neck, my shoulders, my back. And when he reached the flesh of my ass, he nipped at the sensitive skin with his teeth. I squealed out from the sting of it, but he smoothed it better with his lips and tongue.

Hot damn.

His kisses swept up my back again, and when he reached my shoulders, he wrapped his arms around my waist and pulled me tight against his chest.

The hardness of his arousal pressed against my ass, and I moaned.

"I've never been so fucking turned on in my life," he whispered into my ear. "Tonight, I get to kiss and lick and suck and fuck every inch of my beautiful wife. And I'm going to, baby. I'm going to devour every inch of you. And I'm not stopping until neither of us can move."

Oh my and *yes please* were the first and only thoughts to enter my head.

He glided his fingers down my belly until they reached the apex of my thighs. One lone devious finger moved through my arousal, and I moaned.

"So wet. So beautiful. So fucking mine," he whispered into my ear. "I'm going to spend hours upon hours kissing you here, and you're going to come on my tongue."

He slid that provocative finger inside of me. "And I'm going to spend hours in here too. I'm going to slide my cock so deep inside of you, we won't know where you end and I start. Fuck, I'll probably sleep with my cock inside of you, baby."

"God, Levi," I moaned, and I felt his lips crest into a smile against my neck.

"Lie on the bed, baby," he whispered. "I've been waiting what feels like my entire life for this moment, and I can't wait any longer. I need you. All of you. Right fucking now."

He didn't have to tell me twice.

I climbed onto the bed and the instant I was on my back, staring up at Levi, I felt like his hot gaze had the power to ignite my skin into flames.

He slid off his boxer briefs, and I couldn't stop my gaze from moving to his already hard cock. It was big, thick, and jutting out from between his hips, and I licked my damn lips, my mouth craving a taste of him.

He crawled over me, his big, muscular body hovering over mine, and he pressed the head of his arousal just barely against me.

Fuck. I needed more.

I wiggled and moved my hips, but he didn't budge an inch.

"*Now*, Levi," I begged, but he shook his head.

"Not yet," he whispered. "There's something I need to do first."

Do first? What?

I needed him inside of me.

Anything else could wait.

Fuck, everything else could wait.

Armageddon could occur right now, and I still wouldn't want to leave this bed.

"Ivy, you are the light to my dark. The beauty within my soul," he whispered, repeating his vows to me. "Because of you, I'm a better man. You are my lover, my best friend, my perfect match. Every day, for the rest of forever, I want and need your fire and your sass and those big green eyes of yours smiling at me. I want and need your words and your thoughts and quick wit and smart mouth. I want and need every little amazing thing that makes you the strongest, most beautiful woman I've ever known."

He paused to press a kiss to my lips, and my eyes sparkled with emotion.

"Ivy, I promise you, that for the rest of my days, I will love you, care for you, support you, and be the man you deserve. I love you, Ivy. I will never stop loving you."

"God, Levi," I whispered, and a few tears slipped down my cheeks. "I love you so much."

Slowly, oh so slowly, he slid himself inside me until I was filled to the hilt.

I moaned, and he leaned forward to press a slow, deliciously deep kiss against my mouth.

"My wife," he whispered against my lips. *"Mine."*

"Yours."

"Forever," he rasped and slid his cock deeper.

"Always."

I'd never known what it was like to give someone your whole heart and receive theirs in return.

I'd never known love until Levi.

My husband.

Mine. Mine. *Mine.*

9 MONTHS LATER

Levi

Hollywood's elite and a stage covered in what looked like diamonds surrounded us from all sides.

Inside the Dolby Theater, applause rang out as Meryl Streep stepped onto the stage. Her hand gripped the golden envelope that named this year's Oscar winner for best actress.

Ivy sat beside me, four rows from the main stage, and I reached out to grip her hand for support as Meryl Streep smiled at the crowd and started to read from the teleprompter.

I looked at my wife, a little ball of nerves and anxiety and dressed to the nines in a beautiful floor-length black silk gown, and smiled.

She'd spent four hours this morning surrounded by stylists fixing her hair and makeup, and the end result was downright stunning.

Now, I'd still take a just-woken-up Ivy any day of the week, but I could definitely appreciate the mesmerizing vision that was an Oscar-ready Ivy.

Which I hoped was the case in the literal sense.

Because of her amazing performance in *Cold*, she was on the list of five Oscar nominees for Best Actress.

And in mere moments, we were about to find out if she'd go home with a golden Oscar in tow.

"Here are your nominees for Best Actress," Meryl announced into the microphone, and the large screen behind her filled with movie clips highlighting the nominees' award-worthy roles.

"*Ivy Stone in* Cold," rang out from the speakers, and Ivy inhaled a sharp intake of breath.

And then a clip of Ivy in a Cold Police Uniform filled the screen.

She stood inside the Cold police station, and it was a difficult scene where Grace finds out her friend Bethany Johnson had gone missing.

The movie version wasn't quite the same as the real-life version, but it was close, and from the little bit I'd seen of the movie, I knew Ivy had more than done the role of Grace Murphy justice.

For the longest time, Ivy had tried to fight the movie being released, but there was a large part of me that was glad neither of us was successful in that task.

Because, as a result, Grace's story, the victims of Walter Gaskins's story got to be told.

When Ivy and I had gone to the movie premiere for *Cold*, it had been absolute chaos.

It had been a struggle just to get through the red-carpet version of it.

And once we'd stepped inside and the movie started playing, we'd both looked at each other and decided we didn't need to see the final version.

It just didn't matter to us.

We had each other, and in the end, that was all that mattered. Pretty ironic, really, that the only two people in that theater who could have verified how accurate, how fulfilling it was hadn't even stayed to watch it.

"And the Oscar for best actress goes to," Meryl said, and she opened the envelope. The instant she spotted the name, she looked up and smiled toward the crowd. "Ivy Stone in *Cold*."

The room filled with raucous applause, and my jaw damn near hit the floor, and Ivy stayed frozen in her seat for a few seconds, her hands shaking in her lap.

"I won?" she whispered to me, and I stood up.

"You won, baby," I said, and the biggest, proudest smile covered my face. I reached down with both hands and helped my wife to her feet, and then I wrapped her up in a big hug. "You did it, Ivy. You fucking did it. I'm so incredibly proud of you."

She leaned back and met my eyes. "I love you so much."

"I love you too," I said and nodded toward the stage. "Now, go get your Oscar, baby."

A nervous laugh escaped her lips, and I watched her gorgeous little figure slowly make her way up to the stage, fellow actors and actresses stopping her in the aisle to shake her hand and give her hugs as she went.

The entire room was filled with people who felt she deserved this.

I watched in awe as the crowd celebrated my wife.

And, fuck, it was the best feeling in the entire world.

She stepped behind the microphone, and Meryl handed her the Oscar and wrapped her up in a congratulatory hug.

And then Ivy looked at out the crowd, and an emotional smile crested her beautiful lips. She touched the microphone with a shaky hand and took a big, deep breath. "Wow, I'm just...I'm speechless right now," she said. "And a whole lot nervous," she added with a giggle. "So, bear with me here because I'm about to free flow this speech. My husband told me last night I needed to prepare something in case I won, but I just didn't think it was possible. There are so many amazing actresses on that list, and I felt completely humbled just to have been nominated with them, much less actually win. Holy moly," she said, and her eyes went wide. "What is happening right now?"

The crowd chuckled and clapped in response.

God, she was beautiful and so damn adorable it made my chest ache.

"Okay, okay, get it together, Ivy, you're on live television, and now isn't the time to ramble," she muttered more to herself than anyone else, and I grinned.

"This has been a long road for me," she addressed the crowd. "Probably the hardest journey I've ever been on, and to win this award is so bittersweet. I'd like to dedicate this to my beloved sister, Camilla Stone. I miss you every day, Cami. You were the brightest star in the whole sky. The strongest woman I've ever known. And to Grace Murphy. The two of you, both robbed of the beautiful lives you were destined to lead. And if it weren't for you both, I wouldn't be standing here right now.

"I'd also like to thank my husband," she said, and her voice shook with emotion. "Levi, baby, I love you more than should be humanly possible. Thank you for sharing your life with me. And thank you for being the best father to our girls.

"I'd like to thank my parents. Mom and Dad, we did it!" she exclaimed and held the Oscar up. "They couldn't be here tonight because they stayed back to watch our girls, but I know they're watching this at home. Well, unless our one-year-old twins are, like, tearing
their wallpaper down or something. Which, if that's the case, I'm so
sorry, Mom and Dad!"

The crowd laughed again.

"I know there are more names, but I'm just too stunned to process what is even happening right now. So, thank you to everyone
who made this possible. Just…thank you…I'm so humbled and hon-
ored," she said and waved toward the crowd, and everyone stood to
their feet, giving her a standing ovation as she slowly made her way
off the stage.

A few moments later, an attendant came to my row and gestured for me to follow them backstage during one of the commercial
breaks, and the instant my eyes locked with that familiar gorgeous
emerald gaze, my mouth broke out into a huge grin.

Ivy ran toward me, and I wrapped her up in my arms and
hugged her so damn tight that her feet left the ground.

"I can't believe it," she whispered into my ear.

"God, baby, I'm so fucking proud of you."

"I love you," she said and pressed a soft kiss to my lips.

"I love you too, baby," I responded against her lips. We stayed
locked tight in an embrace for a long moment. Eventually, I leaned
back and met her eyes.

"So, now where do we go?" I asked. "After parties?"

She shook her head. "I want to go home, Levi. I want to go
home and see the girls and hug my parents and just be with the people who mean the most to me."

God, I loved her.

And I felt the exact same way.

"But we are definitely picking up some Taco Bell on the way

home because I'm starved," she added, and I burst into laughter.

"What?" she questioned and slapped a playful hand against my chest. "I've barely had anything all day so I could fit into this dress. And now, I'm ready put on some sweats and gorge myself on fucking tacos."

Happy wife, happy life.

I smiled. "Let's go get you some fucking tacos, then."

She giggled, and my heart expanded inside my chest.

To the world, she was Ivy Stone, famous celebrity and, now, Oscar-winning actress, but to me, she was my beautiful, feisty, funny wife who was the best damn mother to our little girls. Ivy *Fox*.

Our life wasn't perfect, but we were blessed. We'd been through hell, and we'd come out the other side more than just intact.

We came out alive and thriving and *together.*

THE END

THANK YOU so much for taking the journey through this trilogy with us. It was different and scary, but in the end, one of our favorite things we've ever done.

We hope we've left your mood right and your heart fulfilled, but if you need some laughs to recover, head on over to our Mavericks Tackle Love Series and start with book one!

Get Wildcat today!

#QBpie #MaxMonroeRomCom #MavericksTackleLove

2018 has been the start of ALL THE FUN THINGS.

Find out why everyone is laughing their ass off every Monday morning with us.

Max Monroe's Monday Morning Distraction.

It's hilarity and entertainment in newsletter form.

Trust us, you don't want to miss it.

Stay up-to-date with our characters, us, and get your own copy of Monday Morning Distraction by signing up for our newsletter: www.authormaxmonroe.com/#!contact/c1kcz

You may live to regret much, but we promise it won't be this.

If you're already signed up, consider sending us a message to tell us how much you love us. We really like that. ;)

Follow us online:
Website: www.authormaxmonroe.com
Facebook: www.facebook.com/authormaxmonroe
Reader Group: www.facebook.com/groups/1561640154166388
Twitter: www.twitter.com/authormaxmonroe
Instagram: www.instagram.com/authormaxmonroe
Goodreads:goo.gl/8VUIz2
Bookbub: www.bookbub.com/authors/max-monroe
Amazon: bit.ly/MMAmazonAuthor

ACKNOWLEDGMENTS

First of all, THANK YOU for reading. That goes for anyone who's bought a copy, read an ARC, helped us beta, edited, or found time in their busy schedule to help us out in any way.

Thank you for supporting us, for talking about our books, and for just being so unbelievably loving and supportive of our characters. You've made this our MOST favorite adventure thus far.

Thank you to Basil and Banana for always being there to keep us in order!

THANK YOU to our amazing readers. Without you guys, none of this would be possible.

THANK YOU to all of the awesome and supportive bloggers. You never hesitate to share our teasers and information, even when it sounds like it's written by someone in the midst of a mental break-down. Thank you so much!

THANK YOU to our editor, Lisa. You are, like, the real deal. You drink wine in our honor (*cough* because of us *cough cough*) and you dominate our deadlines. Thanks for not making fun of us even though we can never ever remember if it should be further or farther.

THANK YOU to our agent, Amy. You never even flinch when we tell you we need something read in a day and a half.

THANK YOU to our Camp Members. You gals are the best-best-best.

WE CAN'T WAIT to SHINDIG with some of you in Denver! #CLY Say whaaaat? ;)

And last, but certainly not least, THANK YOU to our family. We love you guys. Thanks for putting up with us and our moments of creative crazy. Not to mention what feels like a constant state of us looking like hot messes and always on a deadline. Maybe we should stop writing so many books?

Monroe: Yeah, good try. We already have 3 more docs started. You know, Trick Play, and those *other* things.

Max: Why don't you ever sleep?

Monroe: I sleep! Remember, we're taking a whole week off after this.

Max: [rolls eyes] Except for writing. I'm pretty sure we're still going to be writing.

Monroe: Yeah, but come on! It's—

Max: [covers Monroe's mouth]

Monroe: Schillionaire Schmook Schlub?

Max: [closes eyes in despair] I thought we weren't saying anything.

Monroe: [rolls eyes] Relax. We didn't. Not really, anyway. Just enough to make people curious. [looks to readers] Right?

Max: Well, I guess we'll see soon enough. Think this is going to start spreading all over social media?

Monroe: [laughs] Who do you think we are? Beyoncé?

Max: True. I guess we're safe, then.

Monroe: [winks at readers] Of course. Safest we've ever been.

Thank you for reading!
We love you tons and tons and tons!
XOXO,
Max Monroe

Made in the USA
Monee, IL
07 August 2021

75189116R00118